RHINO'S RUN

RHINO'S

RUN

ROBERT LIPSYTE

HARPER
An Imprint of HarperCollinsPublishers

For a hero reader,
Daniel Nachumi

ONE

PUNCHING JOSH KREMENS DIDN'T FEEL AS GOOD AS I thought it would, and I'd been thinking about it for five years. I've even practiced on a punching bag. But the real punch wasn't planned, it was a mindless reaction. He got in my face on a bad day. My hamstrings were sore, which could keep me out of the starting lineup, and I was late on a history paper, which could keep me off the team. Most important, he disrespected a football captain.

Me.

In front of the whole school.

Everybody's seen the videos. After some yelling back and forth, Kremens's big head slammed into my nose, and I swung. A short right. Perfect punch. He's tall and he went down in sections. His knees buckled, his shoulders rolled back, and his body followed his head to the floor. Lucky for him it was thick indoor auditorium carpet. Lucky for me, too. If his head had cracked open, I'd be in deep shit.

Honestly, Ms. Lamusciano, that's all I cared about. The moment before I punched him, I imagined him blocking me from a Division I scholarship. Maybe that's no excuse to you. But if I have to write the truth in this stupid journal, there it is.

Punching Josh Kremens is where this story started, so that's where I'm starting this journal. I'm writing this because you said I have to keep a journal to stay in Group and the principal said I have to stay in Group to stay in school and Coach said I have to stay in school to stay on the football team and I know I have to stay on the football team to make it to a Division I college on an athletic scholarship to get out of this rathole town next year. In other words, to survive.

I'm here with you in Group, Ms. Lamusciano, because I made—in your shrink lingo—a poor executive-functioning decision, self-control division. I slugged Josh Kremens in front of hundreds of smartphone cameras.

This was on a Monday afternoon at the annual Law Enforcement Appreciation Day, a big deal at Woodhaven High School. As I told you already, I was in a lousy mood for starters and there I was, supposed to be all smiley and welcoming, making sure the football team was doing its job of greeting and seating the "dignitaries"—the school officials, town politicians, and every kind of police from the local FBI special agent down to the Woodhaven traffic enforcement officer. That included my dad, an ex-state trooper, who worked security at the community college and the mall.

The football team got the job of being official hosts because the football team always does what it's told, and who else were they going to get when a lot of kids don't like or trust cops.

So the varsity led the dignitaries up onto the stage, while the students filled up the auditorium. As a new co-captain, I was in charge of the opening part of the ceremony, sort of a head monitor. The other co-captain would lead them off the stage at the end. We were in clean red road jerseys, name and number.

I stood in the center aisle, directing traffic, trying to look like I knew what I was doing. I was wearing my friendly face, half-smile, eyes wide open. Once I figured most everybody was seated, I signaled the squad to line up on either side of me and face the audience, back to the stage, arms crossed, as if we were protecting all that firepower behind us from some crazed mob.

Turns out, we were.

The principal, Dr. Mullins, was just tapping the mic when the auditorium's big doors swung open, and Josh Kremens started marching down the aisle toward me at a good pace. He was leading about a dozen kids, one of them beating a drum, others carrying hand-lettered signs, MAKE WAAR—WOODHAVEN AGAINST AUTOMATIC RIFLES.

My first thought was, *Dude has balls, give him that*. My second was, *Not on my watch*.

The team started to move toward them, like it was coming off the line of scrimmage in slow motion. I stepped forward, turned, and motioned the red jerseys back with open palms.

"Hold," I said, like I was talking to my dog, Butkus. Most of the guys stopped in their tracks, but you'd know John Cogan kept moving forward, signaling the players around him, his buddies, the ones he called the Berserkers, to follow him. It's hard for a junior to pull rank on seniors, but I was the captain.

"VIKINGS, HOLD," I shouted.

Amazingly, they held.

Cogan looked surprised. Ever since I was made captain instead of him, he's tried to one-up me on and off the field.

Kremens was halfway down the aisle when I spun around. I marched up to meet him. "Hey, Josh, you'll have to sit down now." I tried to sound friendly. I could feel my friendly face disintegrating. "There are seats in the back."

"Don't block the people. This isn't a game." He had a deep, confident, older voice. Since middle school I've hated that voice, telling people what to do, explaining the world according to Josh.

"You're right," I said. "No game. This is a big deal. We've got guests. We have to show them and the school some respect." I was calm, soft-spoken, like Dad when he tried to defuse tense situations. I loved it when I got to see that.

"Out of our way," he said. It was an order. "We're here to speak truth to power."

That one gets old fast. Whose truth? "You've made your point, Kremens. You can talk to our guests afterward."

"Out of the people's way, Rhino!" his voice boomed. I felt my hands become fists.

"You need to turn around now." I could sense the team coming up behind me, ready for a bloody massacre. Cogan was yelling, "Berserkers, on three!" Bad for everybody.

Kremens lifted a wireless mic to his mouth and shouted, "No justice, no peace."

"Berserkers! One."

The marchers behind Kremens chanted, "No justice, no peace. No justice, no peace."

"Berserkers! Two."

Kremens began reciting the names of schools. By the third one,

Columbine High School, I recognized them as places where kids had been mowed down by assault rifles. I thought, C'mon, not here, not now. Nobody ever got shot in Woodhaven.

Kremens shouted, "Sandy Hook Elementary School!"

I could hear the team breathing and muttering behind me like a beast in a sci-fi movie. It sounded like they were waiting for the signal to charge. The kids with the signs lowered the poles, as if they were spears. They looked serious.

I closed my hand over Kremens's mic. "Okay, we get it. Now, you got to . . ."

He knocked my hand away. The mic fell to the floor. As we both dove for it, he butted me in the face. I stepped back, my eyes going blurry, my nose bleeding.

As his big pale face came up, I threw that sweet short right.

It took him a long time to go down.

The team, the assistant principal, Dad, the school safety officer, swarmed us. Kremens and I were hustled off to the ambulance parked outside school. I was woozy, he looked worse. We didn't talk.

Other than that, Ms. Lamusciano, you can read the reports and watch the videos. It was even on the news.

TWO

WE ATE LATE THAT NIGHT, WAITING FOR DAD TO COME back from meetings at the school and police headquarters. He marched in, scratched Butkus's head, then washed up without talking. He cracked a beer. That's his style, letting the suspense build. My older sister, Alison, says it's his way of getting attention and keeping control. They haven't gotten along in years.

The first thing Dad said when he sat down at the table was, "That was like the phantom punch."

When my younger sister, Livy, asked, "What?" he started to explain how my punch was like the perfect right Muhammad Ali threw to knock out Sonny Liston in the first round of their heavyweight championship rematch in 1965. Dad wasn't born yet, but he remembers the fight like he was in the front row. He's a big Ali fan. Made me one, too. I knew all about the phantom punch.

"The champ was moving forward, and so was Liston," Dad said, his fists floating over his plate, "and the punch was short, so all the velocity went directly to Liston's jaw. Perfect punch."

"Ron?" Mom had her narrow-eyed, tight-lipped, no-bull look on. Her voice was high and strained. She's an all-business real estate agent and doesn't always have the patience to play Dad's games. "Just give us the upshot, please."

"Right," Dad said. He knows when to back off from Mom. "Josh's dad wants blood. Poor little Josh's First Amendment rights were violated, not to mention his jaw."

"What about Ronnie's nose?" Livy asked. She's fourteen, a truly great kid when she's not a pain.

"What do they want?" Mom asked.

"The trifecta. An apology, an assault arrest, expulsion from school."

"No problem with the apology," I said. "I'm very sorry he butted me."

"Right on!" Livy cackled. We fist bumped.

"The butt looked accidental," Dad said.

"Whose side are you on?" Livy asked.

"Justice and peace," Dad said. He heh-hed his little cop laugh.

"Ronnie reacted," Livy said. "He's a jock. No moral delay."

"Moral delay?" Dad shook his head. "Where'd you get that?"

"It means no stopping to think about what you're doing just because it might be wrong."

"That's a psychopath," Dad said.

"Ron?" Mom said. She was getting annoyed. "Anything else you need to share?"

"We're meeting again tomorrow at the school with more people. Cool off. Negotiate."

"What about football?" I asked. "Opening game's on Saturday."

"We'll deal with that," Dad said. "My priority now is to be sure there's nothing on the record that might turn off college coaches."

"Mistake," Livy said. "Didn't you say coaches want players with a mean streak? Otherwise, why do they keep recruiting guys with arrest records?"

"I think you need to be quiet, Olivia," Mom said, "or leave the table. We need to deal with this seriously."

Livy shut up. She wanted in on the story.

"The point right now is damage control," Dad said. He looked at me. "We'll have to figure out how much punishment you're willing to take to achieve your immediate goal, which is to stay in school."

"Stay in school?" It was the first moment I felt anxious.

"Kremens keeps bringing up the school's zero tolerance policy for violence."

"This is ridiculous, Ron," Mom said. "Josh started it. Ronnie was on official duty for the school. He stopped a disruptive act."

"You're right," Dad said. "But Kremens is on the school board and he's running for Town Council, and they're all scared of him. Especially the principal. Her contract's up for renewal."

"What did you mean by 'punishment'?" I asked.

"Kremens kept saying everyone needs to learn that actions have consequences, and you can't be allowed to get off scot-free after attacking another student." He shook his head. "He wants his pound of flesh, and we need to negotiate that down to a few ounces. Damage control."

"Why anything?" Mom said. "Both boys were wrong. Let it go at that."

"This is where we're at right now," Dad said. "Any of that pie left?"

I stood up.

"Where are you going?" Dad asked.

"Some of the guys are . . ."

"Skip it," Dad said. "I want you to lay low. Watch your phone calls. If there really is a lawsuit your phone could be subpoenaed. All we need is a text showing up with you saying something like, 'Yo, bro, it felt so good to crush that snowflake.' It could be entered as evidence to prove malicious intent. Better just clam up."

I wanted to say, C'mon, you've been watching too many cop shows, but I had no energy. My arms and legs felt rubbery. "For how long?" I asked.

"Till the whistle blows. Lift, run, walk the dog. Don't you have a history paper to write?"

"You said it was woke garbage."

"That was then."

Upstairs, in my room, I scrolled through my texts and calls. Most were from guys on the team, telling me to keep my pecker up and work on my left hook for my rematch with Kremens. It was support, what we do for each other, but I didn't answer any of them. Dad had been serious about watching what I said, and it worried me. He might be right. Nothing except football felt safe. Alison said Dad turned paranoid after he resigned from the state police, but sometimes the things that make him suspicious of authority worry me, too.

Like the fact that none of the coaches texted me. Maybe they didn't want their names on the record. Coaches usually never quit bugging you to lift and run and eat right and go to sleep early and stay away from booze and dope and girls and show up on time for the next meeting, blah, blah, blah. Now they were avoiding me. Were they paranoid, too? Or did they know something?

There were texts from Andy Lam, my best friend, and Domi, Justin, and Jamaal, my closest buds on the team. I didn't have the juice to respond.

There was a voice mail from Mr. Biedermann, my history teacher, who doesn't like emails and texts. He prefers looking you in the eye when you talk, but he'll settle for a voice on the phone. He was Alison's favorite teacher, too. I had the feeling my paper was going to be very late. This was no time for a failing grade, even an incomplete. It could affect my eligibility. I called him back.

"Mr. Rhinehart." Mr. Biedermann wasn't really formal, but he didn't pretend he was one of the guys, like some teachers. I respected him for that. But you could still kid around. When I heard crowd noise in the background, I said, "What game you watching?"

"Manchester United and Leicester City."

"Why don't you watch real football?" I asked.

"Why don't you play real *futbol*?" He laughed. "You make any progress with that paper?"

"Not really. I don't think I get this."

"Where are you stuck?"

"Some of the articles you sent me comparing football to slavery. It's your choice to play or not. Guys are making millions."

"You have to be able to deal with the ambiguity here. You have to hold two separate thoughts that seem to contradict each other. You ever hear the phrase 'forty-million-dollar slaves'? It's the title of a book you need to read. All that money, but they're still in the grip of the system.

"And you need to keep the context in mind. More than sixty percent of NFL players are African Americans. But most coaches and almost all owners are white. So, is there any connection between slavery or Jim Crow or even everyday discrimination and the way Black NFL players have been treated, contractually, medically, and in the media?"

My head was bursting. "Can't we get back to block and tackle?"

Mr. Biedermann laughed. "You were the one who wanted to write about football."

"I thought it would be easier than gun control." You can talk straight to Mr. Biedermann.

"Nothing worthwhile is easy."

"But this feels like rewriting history to make some people feel good."

"Sounds like you've been talking to your dad. Better talk to Alison. How's she doing, by the way?"

I didn't want to go there. "She's good."

"Give her my regards. Best student I ever had. Listen, I'll send you some book titles. And I'll extend the deadline by a week. Work for you?"

"I'll try." I wasn't so sure.

"I know you can do it." He clicked off.

I couldn't believe he hadn't mentioned what happened with Josh. I almost wanted to talk to him about it. But then I remembered he was junior class advisor. He might have a vote in any decision about Josh and me, and probably wasn't supposed to talk about it with us. That made me feel a little better.

Andy texted again, this time with a two-minute video titled "Rhino's Greatest Hits." Andy was the audiovisual guy for the athletic department, actually the go-to filmmaker for the whole school. The greatest hits were three of my quarterback sacks and two downfield chase and tackles as a linebacker and the monster block I threw as tight end that sprang Jamaal for his forty-yard touchdown run that won conference last year and, finally, the punch that decked Josh Kremens.

I called him. "It's really good, but you need to keep it to yourself for now."

"What's up?"

"Josh's dad wants my ass. Some kind of negotiations are going on, and Dad has me grounded for the week, low profile."

"Okay. You can use the hit clips, without the punch, when you send your stuff to college coaches."

"That's cool."

"I might want to use the punch in my essay for Mr. Biedermann," Andy said.

"Should be no problem by then."

Instead of a written paper, Andy's doing a video on the importance of varsity football at Woodhaven High. The whole town's obsessed with the team. It seems kind of risky, but Andy has strong opinions on what's right and wrong. Mr. Biedermann is cool with strong opinions. If the vid is good enough, Andy says he'll submit it with his college application next year. I haven't seen any of it yet.

"You okay?" Andy asked. He says it like a partner on a cop show.

"Fine." I don't think I sounded convincing.

"Think Andiron." He clicked off.

Andy and I have had each other's back since elementary school. His dream is to be a great filmmaker, like his hero, Martin Scorsese. He's made me watch Scorsese films like *Goodfellas* and *Raging Bull* dozens of times. He talks about our production company. I'll put up the money with my NFL millions, which is okay with me. Andy even came up with a name—Andiron Productions. Andy-Ron, get it?

We met in fifth grade when we were caught cheating on a math test. The teacher was going to take us both to the principal when Andy confessed that he had been stealing answers from me all year—he just didn't understand math. The teacher didn't believe him. She sat us down after school and went over the test and said she was shocked, a small smart Chinese American kid stealing answers from a big dumb white jock. And then it was a big joke for her. But not to Andy, who said it was racist and happened all the time. He talked about stuff like that back in the fifth grade. We became best friends.

THREE

DR. MULLINS IS A BLACK WOMAN WITH A FRIENDLY personality who likes to roam the halls fist-bumping. She can be tough, although she has a reputation for being fair, especially among jocks. She shows up at all the games and you can always hear her cheering.

Mr. Kremens is a shorter version of Josh with curly gray hair, a little beard, and steel-framed eyeglasses. He was the only one in the conference room wearing a tie. He's some kind of business consultant. He comes across as angry, but it looked like a pose to me. Keep everybody off balance. I try to do the same thing on the defensive line with one of my gargoyle Rhino faces.

Dr. Mullins was standing at the head of the conference table, tapping a ballpoint pen against the wood, when Dad and I walked in. She wasn't scowling, but she wasn't smiling either. She waved us to the opposite side of the table from Josh and Mr. Kremens and we sat down. Mr. Kremens and Dad glared at each other like opposing linemen. Josh and I looked down. Then Dr. Mullins pointed at the door and Mr. Biedermann and a tall red-haired woman I didn't know came in. Her bare, freckly arms were wrapped around file folders and a silver thermos.

"I'm sure you all know Mr. Biedermann. He's here as junior class advisor," Dr. Mullins said. "And this is Ms. Lamusciano, our school psychologist."

Dr. Mullins waited for them to sit down at the far end before she took her seat. It seemed too quiet, almost spooky. The game-day ice ball I'd woken up with grew in my chest.

"Let me say this at the outset," Dr. Mullins said. "I take this incident very, very seriously, and I want to resolve it without litigation or further publicity."

"I hope you don't mean sweep it under the rug," Mr. Kremens said. You could hear where Josh got his deep, confident voice. "One of your students was attacked on school property . . ."

"It was self-defense," Dad said. His voice was higher, sharper, more like a serrated bread knife.

". . . while exercising his First Amendment rights . . ." Mr. Kremens said.

Dr. Mullins held up her hands. "This takes us nowhere, gentlemen. This is not a debate or a negotiation. I called you here to inform you of my decision, made in consultation with the district superintendent, our legal counsel, and Mr. Biedermann and Ms. Lamusciano.

"Josh and Ron will be suspended from school until further notice. Think of it as a cooling down and reflective period, no school-based activities such as sports or clubs allowed. However, they will be required to attend Ms. Lamusciano's alternative group program to avoid the school pressing charges with the police."

"Out of the question," Mr. Kremens said.

"Sounds like a Breakfast Club for delinquents," Dad said.

Dad and Mr. Kremens started talking over each other at Dr. Mullins, who leaned back in her chair looking satisfied, like she'd achieved her goal of pissing off both of them.

Finally, she raised her hands and glared them into silence. "Ms. Lamusciano?"

The school psychologist stood up. She looked friendly but serious. "Woodhaven's ILOD Group is not a Breakfast Club for delinquents," she said. "We meet in the afternoon."

Only Mr. Biedermann laughed. I thought it was funny, but I kept a poker face.

"ILOD?" Mr. Kremens asked, sounding annoyed at not knowing what that stood for.

"In lieu of detention," Dad said in his know-it-all cop voice. "Why would detention be an option?"

"As you are aware," Dr. Mullins said, "criminal charges against both young men are still pending, and they won't be dropped until they successfully complete group counseling."

Dad and Mr. Kremens started talking again, and I began to tune out. I noticed Josh's eyes were glazing over, too. I heard Dad and Mr. Kremens say words like *due process* and *expunging records*, and at first I wondered if they were still sparring with each other like boxers, looking for a weakness, an opening to throw a phantom punch, but then I realized they were now on the same side, protecting their sons by showing they couldn't be pushed around. It's called working the referees, giving Dr. Mullins a hard time so she might not be so tough later on. Did they think this thing was going to drag out?

After a while, everyone else stood up so I did, too. I was in a movie, watching myself. Mr. Kremens stomped out, pulling Josh.

In the car, Dad said, "I'll drop you off home. I have a fill-in shift. I think that went well."

"Went well? Until further notice?"

"We fought for that. Room to negotiate the suspension down."

"Till when? No practice this week. How'm I gonna start?" I hated the whine in my voice. "It's the opener."

"It could have been worse. Suck it up."

"This Group thing?"

"As long as it's not on your record. Coaches hate their players in therapy. They don't want them listening to anybody but them."

Back home, I changed into shorts and a T-shirt and stretched out on my bed. I was tired. Quick nap. I crashed. When I woke up it was midafternoon. Butkus was sprawled out at the end of the bed, waiting for me to play with him. We shared an egg sandwich and played ball in the backyard. Butkus is a lab/shepherd mix and can fetch all day, and I needed to get my body working. He was named after Grandpa's favorite football player, Dick Butkus, the Chicago Bears linebacker, maybe the toughest of all time. Butkus the dog plays with kittens.

As usual, Butkus started barking when I quit throwing the ball to him, and I went into the garage to lift, blasting Machinery, my favorite industrial metal band. That drowned him out. They use jackhammers, leaf blowers, foghorns, you name it. Keeps your blood pounding. I had ESPN on the TV. The coaches want me to lift at school with the team, but sometimes I just don't want to deal with those dumbbells and their trash talk.

Alison says I'm a heavy thinker. Once, she said, "My problem is

I'm a heavy, *heavy* thinker." Not so funny for her. I miss her. I wish she had come home after her freshman year, but I don't blame her. I can tell she's having a tough time in college, but not as tough as she had at home, especially around her weight issues.

I'd like to float this journal business past her, but even after I sent her Andy's "Greatest Hits" clip she didn't get back to me. Every so often she goes into what she calls a communications coma because she's feeling terrific or terrifically depressed and just doesn't want to connect, even with me.

I kind of don't hate the idea of a journal. I've always liked to write. Stories, poems, little essays. I even started some blogs but never sent them out. I have them on my computer, encrypted. Alison is the only one who ever saw them. She says I have writing talent. And not just for a lineman, she said. I even wrote a few mini-documentaries with Andy. He taught me all you have to do is thread your favorite pictures together like pearls on a string with a little narration. It's easier than writing a novel.

"Ronaldo." It was Dad, home early. He got behind me and lifted the bar out of my hands and onto the rack. "Wash up for dinner."

"Not done yet."

"You are." He grabbed a handful of flesh under my triceps and pulled me off the bench.

I pretended it didn't hurt. I'm still trying to figure out whether pretending it doesn't hurt or shaking loose with an angry look is the best way to get him to stop, but I think it doesn't matter. In Psychology, I figured out that Dad was off taking a leak when they distributed empathy. He just doesn't know how other people feel. Or maybe he doesn't care. Great for a cop.

Alison and I talked about that, and she said you couldn't call him a bully because bullies at least have some twisted form of empathy; that's how they know which buttons to push on the people they terrorize. Bullies have enough empathy to understand what other people are feeling, but they also have an override switch so they don't care. Sergeant is worse than a bully, Alison says, he's a mindless brute. A psycho.

I'm not sure she's right about that. I've seen him do nice things, although not recently.

Alison hasn't referred to him as Dad in years. It's always Sergeant, his rank in the army and in the state police.

At dinner, Mom listened to Dad's version of the meeting with Dr. Mullins, which he made to sound like we were on our way to signing a Mideast peace treaty. Dad at his upbeat best.

"What now?" Mom asked.

"We chill, ride out the storm," Dad said. "Everything's going to be fine. While Ronnie serves his suspension this week, he writes his history paper, gets in shape for the game, keeps his eyes on the prize." He slapped my knee, just hard enough to sting. "And goes to Group. Whatever it is, just play their little game."

FOUR

WHATEVER IT IS, I NOW PLAY THEIR LITTLE GAME IN A semicircle in the first-floor conference room, wedged into a one-size-fits-all hard plastic chair supposedly shaped for comfort. But since every chair is the same and every butt is different, some kids slip around like soft-boiled eggs and big guys like me feel stuck in a can. In school, one size fits nobody.

First day, it's obvious that Group is a locker room for losers. But just the way they say *Group*, like *Church* or *Practice* or *Prom*, makes it sound like a sacred activity instead of a dumpster.

I walk in late. First person I spot is Keith Korn, a tall, twitchy guy I've seen in the halls getting tuned up by Cogan and the Berserkers, shouldered, tripped, slammed into other kids. Once, Cogan stuffed him into a locker. Kids say he didn't say a word and showed no expression. But the next day, taped on the glass showcases in the school lobby, covering up the sports trophies, were these cartoons of pigs and crocodiles with the recognizable faces of Cogan and his main buddies on the team, Belfer, Dowling, and Perlick.

Everybody knew it was Keith's work, which immediately solved the mystery of who had been drawing the same kind of stuff all over town, on sidewalks, overpasses, garage doors, mostly caricatures of the mayor and the police chief, as pigs with police batons up their butts. He confessed right away, proud of it, I guess, and got arrested. That's how he earned his in-lieu-of-detention ticket to Group. I felt a little sorry for him getting bullied so much and then getting busted, because he was such a good artist.

He was slumped in a chair when I walked into Group. He sat up and glared at me. He was wearing an oversized sweatshirt with a picture of Malcolm X on his chest. I thought it was pretty cool, but I know it pissed off some of the Berserkers, who were borderline skinheads. Keith liked to provoke people.

"The great Captain Rhino itself." Keith had a high, nasty voice. "Who'd you come to punch?" Nasty but nervous.

I gave him the Rhino Flick, the one I use just before the third-down snap, a quick glare then look away, dismissing the opponent as nothing. I checked back for his reaction. He dug into his pocket and came up with a big black thing that could have been a harmonica or a vaper. It was an inhaler. He took a puff. I felt even sorrier for him. Asthma.

"Welcome, Ronald," Ms. Lamusciano said.

"Welcome, Ronald," echoed everybody in their one-size-fits-nobody chairs. Even Josh Kremens, who was, of course, sitting front row center. With a smirk. I felt like punching him again. Use the left this time. A hook.

"We have two new . . ."

". . . terrorists . . ." Keith said.

". . . members today, so let's introduce ourselves to them." Ms. Lamusciano smiled at me and Josh. "Joy?"

I found a chair in the back. It was so tight I figured it would stick to me when I stood up.

I'd seen Joy in the gym before she came out as trans—a small varsity gymnast, now the first trans athlete in school. Dr. Mullins and the athletic department still hadn't decided if she could compete on the girls' gymnastic team. I haven't really thought about it much. Cogan and the Berserkers think it's a bad idea, like it's their business.

"Hi, I'm Joy Griffin . . ."

"But you're still Black," Keith said.

"And you'll always be an asshole, Keith," Joy said without missing a beat. "I was caught stealing cosmetics at the CVS because I was too ashamed to buy it openly." She smiled. "Now, as I transition with the support of Group, I can buy my products without shame. Thanks to Group." It sounded memorized but still kind of sad.

Ms. Lamusciano led the clapping. "Marco?"

Marco mumbled something I didn't catch. I didn't try too hard. I knew him from football. He was kicked off JV last year after a school security guard found some pills in his backpack. He should have been given a second chance, but he didn't come back. He turned into a big sad sack who hid himself in a dark blue hoodie.

"I work with the cops now, buy cigarettes and beer, then help them bust the store for selling to minors." He didn't sound very proud of it.

"Marco the Narco," Keith said. "Snitches get stitches."

Ms. Lamusciano quickly said, "Tyla?"

I hadn't seen her before. It's not that big a school, around six hundred students, but kids kind of stay in their bubbles. Or maybe she was new. Tall, skinny, with curly dark hair that tumbled down to her shoulders, and coppery skin. Also, nose, ear, lip, and eyebrow piercings. She made me think of Medusa in Greek mythology, who had snakes for hair. If you looked into her eyes, you'd turn to stone. It was called getting Gorgonized. Alison loved that story.

"I'm Tyla Fernandez. I stole some money from an old man," she said. "For drugs." She held her arms, which were covered by long sleeves. Tattoos or needle marks, I figured. "I've been clean for two months."

"So what did you promise the old man?" Keith asked. "Did you come through?"

Tyla stood up. Joy reached out and grabbed her wrist.

"I think it's Josh's turn," Ms. Lamusciano said.

Josh took his time standing up and facing the Group with a big smile. The hero. Cooling the situation. I really need to clock him again. "I don't think any of us should be here. We're prisoners of a political system that makes victims out of—"

"What about Rhino?" Keith asked. "Why's he here?"

"He's a political prisoner, too, even though he doesn't understand that yet," Josh said.

"What do you say, Rhino?" Keith asked. "You just here to punch people, keep 'em in line? What? Can't hear me?" He cupped a hand around one ear.

Ms. Lamusciano said, "Keith. We're here to support each other."

He ignored her. "The brain damage starts early, in peewee." He drew out the words.

I hated peewee football. I was bigger than any of the kids my age, so I had to play with older kids who beat me up. Then my body changed. I hardened up and everything changed. But revenge isn't always as sweet as people who never get revenge think it is. Revenge is never enough.

"Ronald, what did you feel about what Keith just said?" Ms. Lamusciano asked.

Feel? Here we go. The squishy people.

"Keith's right, for once," I said. "I didn't hear a word."

Keith glared. I gave him the Rhino sneer. Standard first down situations. All that hate felt like heat. What was up with this creep?

Joy started talking about how important it was to share our feelings, and Josh agreed, and I shut down. I could tell Group was going to be a total time suck. I started reviewing game plans in my head, fantasizing about phantom punches for Keith, and a second one for Josh.

"We only have a few minutes," Ms. Lamusciano said. "For our newest members, we need to talk about our journals."

"What about Ronald?" Tyla asked. "He hasn't had a chance to tell us about himself."

Everybody looked at me, except Josh. Our eyes hadn't met the whole session.

"We'll save that for next time," Ms. Lamusciano said, "which will be tomorrow. I'm adding an extra session this week because of our new members."

"Now, your journals. They're important. You need to be self-analytical. You need to be making entries in your journals every day, even if it's just one sentence."

"When are you going to read the journals?" Joy asked.

"Maybe never," Ms. Lamusciano said. She took a hit from her silver thermos. I wondered what was in it. "This is something you're doing for yourselves. A commitment to getting connected to yourself. To exploring your feelings, finding out who you are. It's mostly honor system, but I may have to check that there actually is a journal, be it written, audio, video, but I won't actually read them without permission."

"You expect us to believe that?" Keith asked.

"Encrypt it," Tyla said.

"Marco can still sell it to the cops," Keith said.

Marco raised a middle finger. Best he could do. The guy's road-kill.

The bell rang.

Keith slipped out first, then Josh. I let them all go ahead of me. Last thing I want is someone claiming I bumped them. Big guys get that.

Ms. Lamusciano snagged my jersey at the door.

"Ronald?" She had her smile on. "I understand you don't want to be here, but from a selfish point of view I'm so glad you are. As a member of a sports team, a captain, you know more about group dynamics than anyone. You can help me."

I gave her my blank lineman look, the one people expect. Alison calls it the Rhino Glaze.

"I know you're not as dumb as that." She patted my shoulder. "Rhino."

She is cool. Even knows my nickname. Good try. Slick as a coach.

"Thank you, Ms. Lamusciano."

"Call me Ms. L, it's easier. Do you have any questions?"

I wondered why she was trying to play me. I nodded at her thermos. "What are you drinking?"

She laughed. "Green tea. All kinds of health benefits. You should try it."

"Thanks. I will."

She tried to block the doorway, but I juked around her.

"You down with the journal?" she called to my back.

"Down with"? Is that how she thinks I talk? Did she read it in *How to Communicate with a Dumb Jock*?

"I relate positively to the graphic content," I replied over my shoulder.

I liked her laugh. But I didn't trust her.

FIVE

DINNER WAS JUST ME. MOM WAS AT AN OPEN HOUSE, Livy was at a preseason basketball clinic, and Dad had a tour at the college before a late shift at the mall. He was taking on all the work he could lately. Mom said he was worried about money, although he never mentioned it. I wondered if he needed to get out of the house, to feel like a cop, even a flashlight cop. Or maybe it was because Mom was the big breadwinner these days, although she never brought it up. I think that bugs him. Part-time college and mall cops don't earn much. Or get much respect. Meanwhile, Mom's on her way to a broker's license and her own real estate agency someday.

But she's still Mom. She left me a big salad with a potato, broc, and a steak to heat up. Linemen need protein and carbs, but I didn't have much of an appetite. Just two days into my suspension, and it felt like my system was slowing down.

After I walked and fed Butkus, he conked out on the living room couch. I'm the only one who allows him on the couch. And then he tries to take up the whole thing.

There was a voice mail from Mr. Biedermann. "Get those books yet? You can borrow mine."

I was glad to be able to text back, **Got 'em**. I'd found them in the town library's county share program and had them sent directly to my Kindle. I got the Kindle two birthdays ago from Alison. She was determined to keep me reading after she left. It worked. Of the books she loaded on it, the one I liked best was *East of Eden* by John Steinbeck, who became my favorite author, especially after I read *The Grapes of Wrath* and *The Red Pony*. Sometimes I get a little lost in his nature descriptions, but you got the sense he really understood people and cared about them.

The books I got from Mr. Biedermann's list were *Forty Million Dollar Slaves* by William C. Rhoden, a big-time sportswriter I'd seen on ESPN, and *A People's History of Sports in the United States* by Dave Zirin, who had a column I read sometimes.

I like reading a book on a Kindle screen—the lighting's good, although it's hard to underline and take notes, which I don't like to do anyway. I started with Rhoden's book since it said he had played defensive back at a Division I college. He didn't have any tips for me, but the book got my attention quickly. I lost track of time.

Hey, Ms. L, I bet you didn't know that the first great athletes in America were enslaved Black boxers, rowers, runners, and jockeys who competed for their owners against other plantations. Also bet you're not that interested. But this is my journal. Once there was big money to make in sports, white athletes took over. They pushed out the Black jockeys and rowers, kept pro football and especially baseball lily white for many years, and even though there were always lots of Black boxers, there was no Black American heavyweight champion until Jack Johnson in the twentieth century. He reminded me of Muhammad Ali. I have to tell Dad, who thought Ali was a great boxer and a courageous Parkinson's disease patient but not such a great American for refusing to be drafted. Gramps was a Joe Frazier fan. No surprise there. But Dad can surprise you sometimes. He's not predictable.

Livy was the first one home. She did a comical double take when she saw me with my Kindle on the couch.

"You can read?"

"It's Butkus's book. How'd you do?"

"I don't think I'm even going to get to try out. Coach hates me."

"Why?"

"I don't know. He yells at me more than anybody, every little thing."

"Maybe he thinks you're worth the extra attention. That you're good enough to get even better."

She grinned and her eyes got big. "You really think so?"

"No. I hate you, too."

She gave me a hug and headed upstairs.

"You have dinner?" I asked.

"We went for pizza."

I kept reading. I wanted to skip ahead to the college football section but kept finding interesting stuff.

Mom looked pleased to see me reading, gave me a thumbs-up. Dad wrinkled his nose at the title.

"It's pretty good, Dad. Did you know that—"

"This is all about trying to rewrite history and load white people with guilt." He poked at the Kindle. "Some college professor write this? Did she ever go to a football game?"

"He's on ESPN, played Division One ball."

That was a sore point with Dad. He got hurt his senior year in high school, never got to play in college. "He drank the Kool-Aid."

I should have just shrugged. Control. But I felt like I needed to stick up for Mr. Biedermann. "He makes some good points. Most NFL players are Black, and they still get discriminated against. They even got screwed on the brain trauma settlements."

"Christ, you're starting to sound like your sister." Dad was getting steamed.

I backed off. "I haven't talked to Alison in a couple of months."

"I never do unless she wants money."

Now I needed to stick up for Alison. "Give her a break, she's trying."

"Give me a break. Read that baloney if it'll keep you on the team." He went into the kitchen for a beer and took it downstairs to his man cave. Alison calls it the precinct house because of all the police patches on the walls.

I tried to read some more, but I'd lost it yammering with Dad. After a while I headed upstairs. With no school, I could sleep late, till they were all gone.

But I couldn't zonk out, like I usually do. I started thinking about football and my mind drifted into my old daydream of Rhino's Run.

Every time I dreamed about The Run it was a little different except it always started with an interception by me. It seemed more dramatic, a linebacker making a pick to turn a losing game around. This time we were in a suicide blitz, everybody charging the quarterback, only I hung back two steps because I sensed he was going to roll left, fake, then spin to his right to target his favorite wideout. I was ready. His pass slammed into my chest. I hung on and went downtown.

Rhino was an express train rumbling down the field, batting tacklers out of his way, running them over until the field was empty. He lifted off the ground, light as a paper airplane. Rhino was flying.

He was in the end zone, and everyone was standing, cheering, even Cogan and the Berserkers.

The next morning, I took Butkus for a run through the neighborhood. Butkus was glad I was on suspension, more hanging out together. Then back to the book until it was time for Group.

When I got there, Josh was in a serious discussion with Joy. She was smiling and nodding at him. I heard Josh say "Strong woman" and "Stand up for what you believe." I must have grunted too loudly because Josh shot me a cold look. I squeezed into the farthest chair from him.

Tyla caught my eye, smiled. "I'm looking forward to your introduction today."

"I am Rhino. I hit people," Keith said in an Arnold Schwarzenegger voice. I may have been the only one who laughed. Keith was wearing a Hillary Clinton sweatshirt. Berserkers are going to love that one, too.

"We need to be talking about working together," Josh said. He was trying to take over Group.

"Let 'em fight," Joy said. "It's what boys do when they can't think or feel."

"That why you switched teams?" Keith asked.

"That's stupid," Joy said, "and proves my point."

"You don't have a point anymore," Keith said. "Or do you?"

"Not cool. Not helpful," Josh said. "We need to be fighting the people who stuck us here."

"Hi, everybody, sorry I'm late." Ms. L came and dropped her thermos and folders on her desk.

We arranged our chairs and sat down. Once we got going I could drift away. One session and I already knew the drill. Hey, as a member of a sports team, I know more about group dynamics than anyone, right? Ms. L would open with a question and Joy and Tyla would pick up on it and Marco would just sit there like a loaded Hefty bag and Josh would try to steer the discussion into something he wanted to talk about and Ms. L would let it go on too long while Keith would glare at me and I would ignore him, creeped out and wondering how I had ever got onto his radar in the first place. Why does he hate me? I never bullied him. Of course, I never stopped Cogan and the Berserkers either. Not my business. Keep your eyes on the prize. I'm captain of the football team, not captain of the whole school.

"Ronald?" It took a few beats before it registered.

"Brain-dead, nothing to say," Keith said.

"Ron never says anything," Tyla said, "unless he has something to say." How would she know?

"That true, Ronald?" Ms. L asked. I realized everybody was look- ing at me.

"It's Rhino, not Ronald," Keith said. "His name is Rhino."

He reached into his backpack and pulled out a sketchpad. The picture was good, the face on the rhinoceros's body looked like me, even with a horn where the nose should be. There was a second horn, bloody, sticking out of the rhinoceros's butt.

"You like it, Rhino?" Keith asked. "Feels good, like the locker room?"

"You're sharing your pain, Keith," Ms. L said. "That's good."

"Sharing with him?" Keith spat it out. "He's a jock. He lives to give pain. That's why he's here."

"Maybe he needs support, too," Ms. L said.

"Rhino shouldn't be here," Keith said.

"Why?" Ms. L asked.

"Because he's the problem, one of the people who prey on other people, who . . ."

"This is ridiculous," Tyla said. "What did he ever do to you?"

"You standing up for Rhino?"

"I think we should call him Ronald here, or Ronnie," Tyla said. "He's here to get away from being Rhino."

"Could you unpack that for us?" Ms. L asked.

"Rhino's a brute name," Joy said. "His football name. His teammates and people who don't like him call him Rhino. It's a way of dehumanizing him."

She reached out to give me a little punch on the shoulder. I have to admit that got to me a little. I nodded to her. Ms. L was nodding. The Group clapped, everyone except Keith, who blew a mouth fart.

"Let's get back to Ronald," Ms. L said. "How do you feel about being called Rhino?"

I shrugged as if I never thought about it, didn't care. Don't show any weakness. I got called Rhino in peewee when I was the biggest, slowest, fattest, clumsiest kid on the team. I hated the name. Alison tried to convince me it was okay; it was only because our name was Rhinehart, she said, but I knew that wasn't totally true.

After the fat hardened into muscle, I wasn't always the biggest anymore, but I wasn't slow or clumsy either. And my Rhino horn was my strong right arm, and my Rhino skin was armor that protected me from insult. Don't mess with Rhino. I've never liked the name, but I've come to appreciate its power, even come to depend on it.

"Ronnie?" Tyla was staring at me.

"We all have nicknames on the team," I said.

She gave me a smile, like she knew what I was doing. Alison calls it deflecting. Brushing off a tackler with words. Tyla was reading me. Somehow that didn't turn me off.

"This is avoiding the larger issues," Josh said. "The power structure wants us to think we create our own problems when it's their political, educational, chemical pollution that causes most of our problems."

"Right on," Keith said. "Climate change makes you talk too much." For a total douche, Keith could be smart and funny.

"And like all existential issues pits us against each other," Josh said.

"Climate change is important," Ms. L said, "but so are our individual issues. Ronald never got to introduce himself last time."

Everybody turned to look at me.

"He's just a jock fascist," Keith said, "born to dominate and control and hurt other people. What else do we need to know?"

"Ronald?" Ms. L asked.

I needed a deep breath. "I'm a football player," I said, "and I'm here because I have to be here if I want to stay on the team. That's my story."

Perfect timing. The bell rang.

SIX

SUSPENSION SUCKS. I'M GOING STIR-CRAZY. I'M
stretching and lifting and running too much, not doing my hammies any good. Butkus is exhausted. He starts to slink away when he
sees me come for him with his leash.

Keeping up with schoolwork is easy. The teachers are good about
emailing assignments and homework, and between Andy and Justin
I get the class notes. AP Literature was easy, I'd even read two of the
books, *The Great Gatsby* and *Catcher in the Rye,* and I was ahead of
the class in AP Bio and Precalc. French would need some catch-up
even if I was there. *Mange merde* is all I can ever remember.

Without football and classes the only other people I see are at
Group. Amazing how fast something brand-new becomes routine.
It's like a sitcom you never really liked, sorry Ms. L. Or maybe
a tryout for one. Call it *Not Friends.* Josh trying to run the show,
Keith trying to act like the world's biggest asshole (he's going to get
the part!), Marco like a garbage bag waiting for pickup, Ms. L like a

touchy-feely shrink. Tyla and Joy seem like real people. And I'm just there, pretending to be invisible. Too big for that.

I almost wished I was into social media to make time pass—Facebook, Instagram, Twitter—but Alison kept me off them as a waste of time and a way of getting into trouble. I checked in now and then, along with a little porn, but most of the time I felt too guilty to stay on long. There are a couple of football sites I visit, and that helps.

Football is king at Woodhaven. I should know, being third generation. Even my grandfather has that Viking pride that the coaches pumped into us. We're constantly told we're better than anybody else. Alison says that coaches keep saying it because they need to delude themselves into believing how powerful they are. How else can they beat on teenagers to win games for them and then go jump to a better-paying coaching job somewhere else? That's how Alison thinks.

I had a kind of revelation about coaches and football my freshman year when the drama teacher asked if I could help move props during the school play. I liked the drama kids, they worked together, helped each other out, trusted each other as much or more than football players did. And they partied hard!

I got onstage in the spring play, a singing sailor in *South Pacific*. I loved it. But Coach said I'd have to choose. No distractions allowed.

The opener was an away game, and since I couldn't even be on the sidelines because of the suspension, I stayed home. Andy came over afterward to show me clips from the game, which we lost, a squeaker, 13–10.

"They needed you, Ron. Cogan is slow and dumb."

"Thanks. Like it's my fault now."

"I didn't mean it that way." He reached over to punch my shoulder, but I pulled away. I didn't want sympathy.

Didn't know what I wanted.

"Coach say anything?"

Andy shook his head. "Cogan made some crack about 'Where's the captain?' and Coach ignored it." He checked his phone. "It's Coach. Gotta go."

I was feeling lonely. I wondered if they were going to let me stay captain. The *C* on my uniform was a very big deal and kind of a stunner.

I know this is over your head, Ms. L. So, some backstory.

First of all, at Woodhaven, the next year's co-captains, rising seniors, are announced at the big varsity dinner at the end of spring practice. But last summer, when the incoming captain unexpectedly moved with his family, Coach appointed me, a rising junior. Cogan was pissed off he wasn't the replacement, and that widened the split between seniors and juniors, not to mention him and me.

I loved being a captain. I'd dreamed of it, but not like this. I wanted to get it the usual way, after a great junior season, having really earned it, not as a way to motivate jerks like Cogan. Dad said not to worry, college recruiters would be very impressed if I helped whip the team into a winner.

And then, first thing I do as captain is punch Josh and get suspended. How cool is that?

SEVEN

THE SECOND WEEK OF SUSPENSION IS DRAGGING EVEN slower than the first. Every day without a word from Dr. Mullins makes it less likely I'll be playing on Saturday, the first home game. I can't miss two games in a row.

Believe it or not, Ms. L, I'm almost looking forward to Group, just to get out of the house.

Almost. Keith bugs me. Why is he on my back all the time? Not that the rest of them are such champs. Josh is definitely trying to take over. Marco's rolled himself into a pathetic lump. Joy has some spirit, she's a jock, but I don't know much about being trans. Can't be easy in Woodhaven.

I can't figure Tyla out—she can be snotty or nice. She's her own person for sure. Kind of interesting.

I sit at the end of the semicircle trying to disappear, which is kind of ludicrous. I avoid letting you make eye contact, Ms. L, and drag me into conversation. Doesn't always work. Like yesterday, you said, out of the blue, "You never got to properly introduce yourself, Ronald."

I mumbled something about being Ronald George Rhinehart III, a junior, a football co-captain.

"Captain Rhino," Keith said. "Special delivery from Cogan."

What did he mean by that?

I almost asked him.

"We should call him Ronald here," Ms. L said. "Or Ron. Which do you prefer?"

I shrugged.

"Moving right along," Josh said. He started talking about a demonstration in another town he was going to. He had room in his car. Ms. L dialed him back, and I was able to tune it all out.

Read, work out, walk the dog, repeat. I even read over this journal. Like around thirty-two pages so far. Pretty sloppy. In some places it reads like a diary, in others a letter to you, Ms. L, and sometimes like I'm actually trying to write a story with all those quotes, which obviously aren't exact. I have a good memory, but, hey . . . I'm glad it's not going to be graded by an English teacher. Grammar, spelling, sequence of tenses, forget it.

My ex-girlfriend, Madison, called to remind me about some party I'd promised weeks ago to attend, Vikings Against Cancer at the hospital. She said she had checked with Dr. Mullins's office, and I was okay to go despite the suspension. She asked about my "mental state."

"Other than going batshit?"

She laughed in a sympathetic way. "It must be hard not playing."

"Yeah." I suddenly didn't want to talk about it, especially with her. Football was one of the reasons we broke up. She loved my being on the team, which made us a big couple on campus, but she thought we should be together more, that I didn't need to work out so much and watch game films on my own. That I was avoiding her. Maybe I was. That I wasn't sharing what was going on in my head. That was true. Out of bounds. I really didn't want her in my head. Or anybody.

"Well . . ." We drifted into goodbyes and take cares.

Andy calls every day, fills me in on the team. I like the idea that they need me, and I feel guilty for not being there. Am I being arrogant thinking I could have made a difference in the last game?

Andy dislikes Coach, especially for pushing us to train and play harder by stoking the competition *within* the team, making us compete for our positions almost on a weekly basis, instead of trying to mold us into a cohesive unit against our opponents like most successful coaches do. That lets Cogan and the seniors concentrate on themselves instead of helping us juniors improve. It's understandable since this is their year to shine and make their college deals, but it was a selfish tactic that was backfiring. A team that wins gets lots more attention from recruiters.

Maybe we need a team psychologist, Ms. L.

I decided to sneak down to the field on the way to Group to see what was going on. I dug up one of Alison's humongous hoodies, which smelled of Butkus, sweat, old food, and weed. But it was big enough even I could hide inside it.

Andy, who was shooting practice with three remote smart phones, spotted me. He knew I wasn't supposed to be there, so he took his time coming over, pretending he was shooting as he backed toward where I lurked under the grandstand.

"Going to call later, got some news," he said. "That Wake Forest thing?"

"It came through?" Some good news for a change. Andy was up for a summer fellowship in the documentary film department at Wake Forest University in North Carolina. Doing well there could be his ticket to Stanford or NYU for college, his first choices. Both have major documentary film departments.

"I'm in if they like my entry. I have to send them a short film."

"You got something?"

"I'm working on something. Want to talk to you about it. Tonight? Uh-oh." He suddenly hunkered down. "Coach Dixon."

The offensive coordinator had spotted me. Some disguise. He came over and squeezed my guns. "You're lifting, Rhino, good man. How's that Group thing going?"

"I'm going."

"We know that. Don't let them mess with your head." Then he slapped my head and jogged back to practice. "Back to work, Lammie."

Andy mimicked a phone call to me and followed Coach Dixon.

It was a light, no-pads practice, but there was just enough banging on the field to get my juices pumping. I wanted to be part of it. Missing opening home game was going to hurt.

As practice wound down, I tried to slip away before anybody else spotted me. My cell beeped. A text from the head coach. Meet him in his office right away. Dixon must have told him I was around.

I got there first, just stood looking at a wall of photos of him with NFL players and famous college coaches. He finally came in and dropped into his swivel chair but left me standing on the other side of his desk, staring at the trophies on his wall. I'd never been alone with Coach before.

"You're not supposed to be here."

I shrugged, trying to come up with an answer.

He did it for me. "You couldn't stay away. I like that, Rhino. Commitment to the program. Talk to me about Group."

I thought of what he wanted to hear. "Touchy-feely bs."

He nodded me on.

"Coach Dixon told me not to let them mess with my head."

"Good advice. Don't forget you're a football player. Your job is to suck it up and execute. You got that?"

"Yes, sir."

"That's the ticket—yes, sir; yes, ma'am; do whatever you need to do to get through it. You remember what I said to you when I made you a captain?"

"To control a team you first have to control yourself."

"That's right. Why did I say that to you?"

"Because everybody's strength is their weakness." How many times had he said that to the team? I didn't like being a parrot, but I was doing what I needed to do.

"Very good. That punch. I know where it came from, believe me I understand, but it was a fool's move. A loss of control. On the field, there'd be a penalty that could cost us the game."

"Won't happen again."

"Better believe it. Dr. Mullins doesn't want you playing this week. She says it sends the wrong message."

I felt that in my stomach. Had trouble keeping my head up.

"I don't agree with her, Rhino. That punch was a mistake, but it came out of good intentions. I think I can talk her into letting you play this Saturday. We have a Vikings tradition to uphold."

He stood up like he was going to pledge allegiance. "The team, the school, the town is depending on you, Rhino." He paused.

"I'm ready," I said.

"I know you've been working out. But where's your head? Can you keep your fists in your pocket, know what I mean?"

"Yes, sir." I felt a jolt of electricity. I was back on the team.

He waved me out of the room with his fist.

EIGHT

MS. L AND MOST OF THE GROUP WERE STANDING IN
front of the conference room when I got there a few minutes late. I
stayed at the end of the line a few feet out of smelling range. Alison's
hoodie stank.

Ms. L was thumbing her phone.

I asked anybody, "What's up?"

"We've been kicked out of our room," Tyla said. "For the debate
team."

"Dr. Mullins is giving them a little send-off," Ms. L said. "They're
going to the state championships."

"Get the debate topic," Josh said. "Resolved: In the United States,
social media is beneficial for democratic values."

Ms. L said, "I'm going to have to leave Keith a note where we'll
be." She reached into her bag and came up with a yellow Post-it pad.
She wrote on a little square sticker and peeled it off.

"Where are we going?" Joy asked.

"The day care center in the basement," Ms. L said. "No one's using it right now."

"Day care," Tyla said. "Perfect."

Ms. L slapped the Post-it on the glass door of the conference room and raised her arm. "Let's go, guys."

I stayed at the end of the line. I didn't have a plan, I didn't even think about it, just waited until everybody else had turned the corner before I reached up as I walked past and pulled the Post-it off the glass. Pure reaction. No moral delay. I crumpled it and stuck it in a pants pocket. I don't think anyone saw me do it. *Group is better without Keith,* I thought. *I'll feel better without that creep around.*

The last time I was in the day care center was freshman year when one of the junior linebackers took a couple of us down to see his baby daughter. He was proud of her, hugged and kissed her. Cute kid. Dr. Mullins closed the center the next year because the school board said it promoted teen pregnancy. There was a fuss and Mr. Kremens threatened to sue, but nothing happened except he got elected to the board. The little furniture and toys were still there. They hadn't figured out what to do with the room.

Giggling, Joy and Tyla played catch with a stuffed animal.

I sat down on a trunk filled with blocks. It was even less comfortable than the one-size-fits-none chairs upstairs.

"We'll give Keith another minute or two," Ms. L said.

"He can have as much time as he wants," Tyla said. "Like forever."

I couldn't resist winking at her. She smiled back.

"I think we need to cut him some slack," Josh said. "You can tell he's got some real issues."

"You think?" Tyla said.

"We're all in this together," Josh said. "The point of Group is Ms. L helping us help each other."

"That's very well said, Josh," Ms. L said. "What do you think, Ronald?"

I surprised myself. "I think Josh has a point." I wondered if I meant it, or it was something I figured would get back to Coach and to Dr. Mullins. Rhino is down with the program. You can count on him. Keep him eligible. Or was it another wink at Tyla?

"You know what I think?" Joy said. "Being sent down here shows what the school thinks of us."

"What's that?" Ms. L asked.

Josh jumped in. "It doesn't matter what they think. We're here to figure out who we think we are."

He was taking over. Just like he tried to do in every class since sixth grade, when I started imagining punching him. I felt a combination of anger, admiration, even some of the competition I felt with Cogan. I was surprised at how easily it bubbled to the surface. I usually do a better job of keeping it buried, even from myself.

"I've figured out that I'm tired of your bullshit, Josh," I said.

There was a sudden silence in the room, which made the shots sharp and clear.

"Firecrackers?" Joy asked.

I knew right away it was a short burst from a Colt AR-15. I'd heard the sound often enough on the firing range with Dad. It was coming from a room upstairs. I knew what to do. Dad had drilled me on that, too. I slammed the door shut with my shoulder and locked it, yelling, "Down, everybody down."

Except for Marco, who was frozen, everybody hit the floor. Joy and Tyla pulled him down. Ms. L was crouched in a corner, on her phone.

I started dragging the teacher's desk toward the door. Josh crawled over and pushed until we had the door blocked.

The gunfire stopped. For a moment, I hoped it had been sound effects from YouTube. I'd heard that, too.

Then the screaming began.

There was a single shot.

Miss me, Ms. L? The next few days were weird and blurry. Been too hard to sit and write till now. Anyway, most of what I remember is from watching TV, cops charging in, hustling us out of the building and down to the football field, where we waited for our parents. It looked like every other school shooting on TV. Girls crying, guys looking like they were afraid they would, too. I felt numb and, when I heard the news, sick to my stomach.

Keith was the shooter. According to kids who were there, he burst into the conference room yelling and waving an AR-15 before he realized the Group wasn't there. He started backing out without shooting, but Dr. Mullins rushed him, and he fired a burst over her head. The bullets ricocheted off the walls and hit her and four kids. Nobody died. None of the wounds were life-threatening.

Then Keith put the rifle up to his head. He was crying and saying, "I'm sorry, I'm sorry."

He fired one shot. It grazed his scalp.

At home that night, Mom and Livy couldn't stop crying and kissing me, but after he gave me a bear hug, Dad just shook his head. He'd been at the college when it happened, raced over, and helped clear the school. He said he thought the Woodhaven cops were slow charging in. He wondered why Keith attacked the debate team. He said he wished he was in charge of the investigation instead of the town's dumbass chief who only cared about Woodhaven's reputation and his own.

I barely ate dinner and went upstairs early. Mom knocked on my door a couple of times asking if I was okay but didn't push it when I said I was fine.

I felt way down. It was my fault. People would figure out eventually that Keith was coming after Group. They'd blame Ms. L for not letting him know where we were meeting. After they found out about her Post-it, they'd wonder what happened to it.

I dug the yellow square out of my pocket, uncrumpled it, and tore it into tiny pieces. I flushed it down the toilet. I felt worse. Coward.

I tried to look at it another way. You saved the Group. He was probably coming to kill us. And then another way. Maybe if Keith had come into our room, Ms. L could have talked him out of shooting, maybe I could have jumped him.

I couldn't sleep. I started rereading this journal, which seemed even worse than last time I reread it, a badly written piece of crap by a chickenshit clown. I thought about destroying it, but that's when I decided to put in about tearing off the Post-it. Probably a stupid idea, but it made me feel better. It was the truth. I don't expect anyone will ever read this, but it keeps the journal honest. I don't know why I think that matters, but I do. If I'm honest in the journal, I'm at least being honest with myself.

The school stayed open through the weekend. It sent invitations to come talk with teachers and special counselors. As a captain, I shared that on the Vikings chat pages as an example for some of the younger players who might think that ballers didn't need help. The girls were still crying, and guys comforted them while trying to cop feels. Even Madison and I hugged in the hall, but there seemed to be something phony about it. They were show hugs. In the auditorium there were endless pep talks from coaches, guidance counselors, even the mayor. The janitors and cafeteria staff came in to tear down the decorations for the party after the home opener.

I was amazed to find out that there had actually been a discussion over whether to cancel the game. Seemed like a no-brainer—who wanted to play a game, much less dance or hang out? But some parents and teachers thought it was important to show Woodhaven was too strong to be stopped. Most thought it was more important to respect the wounded and cancel. With Homecoming coming up in three weeks, there would be time to party then. I wondered where Dad and Mr. Kremens stood. Dad had extra security shifts at the mall and the college. They were afraid of more shootings, like it could be a flu that was going around.

On Sunday, Cogan and the Berserkers paraded around the school and through the halls with WOODHAVENSTRONG! banners the art teacher had students make. Andy filmed them. He told me it was Dr. Mullins's idea. She had assigned Andy to make a short documentary called *WoodhavenStrong!* showing the school bouncing back from the shooting. Crazy. We haven't bounced back yet. Andy thought it could be his Wake Forest entry if it wasn't too cheesy.

Josh and his social warriors showed up with their MAKE WAAR signs. There was some yelling and shoving, but the cops separated them from the Berserkers and then they chased the gun control kids. I shadowed Andy, making sure nobody tried to block his cameras.

NINE

ON MONDAY, DR. MULLINS SHOWED UP ON SKYPE FROM her hospital room. We would come out of this better people, a better school, she said. WoodhavenStrong!

Big surprise that night. A sign of life from Alison! She texted **U K?**

That was an upset.

I texted her right back, then every couple of hours for two days. No answer. Sent a few emails, wrote her what happened. I even called, leaving a voice mail. Nada. Typical. I'm almost thinking of you, baby bro, over and out. That's her style.

I thought about driving upstate to visit her. Since she responded to the shooting, I wondered if I could do something like that. But Coach texted he was counting on me to help lead the team through "the situation." That was the word he used, *situation*, like it was a minor problem, say, unlaundered jerseys before a big away game. Hey, it's not as if Keith shot up the football team.

I finally justified not going up because of Alison's thing about privacy. Walk into her room without knocking, there was a good chance something hard would come flying at your head. Even if you knocked and didn't wait for her "Come," which might never come. Happened to me more than once. Lucky I have good reflexes.

Breaking news! Alison called me back.

"I babysat Keith Korn once," she said without even saying hello. "Weird. Sweet. Sad. But some bad stuff was going on in that house."

"Like what?"

"Abuse for sure. Physical, emotional. Dad was a monster. Made Sergeant seem like Mr. Rogers."

"I think Keith was coming after me. Or at least this therapy group they made me join."

"Therapy group?" She sounded interested.

"For punching Josh Kremens."

"Why'd you do that?"

"It's a long story. How are you?"

"Just making sure you're all right." She hung up.

That was a great call, believe it or not, Ms. L.

The shooting was just a blip on the national news, I guess because nobody died. And it didn't last much longer on the local news. Bad for real estate, according to Mom. She was back in all-business mode once she decided I was okay. Dad was more involved in the side effects of the situation, law enforcement getting together to plan for the next shooting. I just went back to classes, figuring suspension was over. So did Josh. Nobody said anything about it, which didn't surprise me. People were thinking about the shooting. The punch was ancient history.

Ms. L was visiting classrooms, meeting with individual kids and teachers, different clubs and organizations. There were grief counselors you could go to, but nobody I knew went. When I mentioned to Coach that no jocks were getting checked out, he asked me to set up a meeting with Ms. L. She looked impressed when Coach asked me, as a captain, to introduce her to the team. I'm not much of a public speaker, but I think I did okay.

"Listen up, guys," I said, getting my voice as deep and loud as I could, Josh-style. We were in a kneeling circle in the locker room. "Ms. Lamusciano is the school psychologist, and as you know I go to her Group, so I can tell you she can be really helpful. Let's give her a Viking welcome and pay attention to what she says."

There was a round of applause and then the guys settled in. If fifty pairs of eyes undressing her bothered Ms. L, she didn't show it.

"Thanks, Rhino, I appreciate that vote of confidence. And thank you, Coach, for inviting me. Gentlemen, I won't take much of your time. Compared to other school shootings, you could say we got off easy: no one died, no one was seriously injured. But it was still a traumatic experience.

"I know a lot of you have heard about PTSD from returning vets, maybe in your own families. Memories of combat come back to haunt even the toughest men and women, sometimes in unexpected ways, through noises like fireworks and cars backfiring, even TV shows and movies.

"Well, we've been through combat here, and it's not going away so quickly, and for some of us it never will. It may be even tougher on you guys than, say, the drama club, because you've been taught to be stoic, not to show pain, to suck it up, to walk it off."

She let that sink in. I could tell they were getting into it. I was impressed.

"Well, you can't walk it off. You have to try to talk it off, share your pain, especially with someone experienced in dealing with it. One thing to avoid"—she smiled and raised an eyebrow—"is self-medication, alcohol, painkillers off the street, and recreational drugs, which usually make it all worse."

She talked some more, gave out her office hours and contact numbers, then asked for questions. I figured there wouldn't be many, if any. We jocks don't like to let on we don't know everything.

But Cogan's hand shot up. "So what's with the shooter, that creepy Korn kid?" He got sniggering laughs from the Berserkers. "Lurch couldn't even find his own brain."

Ms. L's eyes got cold, but she didn't change her expression. "Keith is in the hospital with non-life-threatening head injuries and will be psychologically evaluated."

"He was in your Group," Cogan said, accusingly, I thought. "What was his problem?"

"Even if I could tell you that, I wouldn't," she said. "It's confidential information. I'd never reveal anything about you if you came to me."

"Dream on for that," Cogan snapped. "Aren't you supposed to pick up on somebody like him, a weirdo ready to blow?"

I stepped into the kneeling circle. "Any other questions?"

Cogan shouted, "I'm still . . ."

"All we have time for," Coach said, clapping. "Thank you very much, Ms. Lamusciano."

She got an even bigger round of applause.

On his way out, Coach gave me a thumbs-up.

A couple guys came up, grinning, and asked me how they could get into Group. I told them to jack a 7-Eleven. Laughs.

I was feeling good until Cogan shouldered me in the hall. "Don't you ever interrupt me, Rhino."

"You were out of line."

"You talking to me?"

"You deaf as well as stupid?"

He moved toward me, but his chief bobo, Perlick, pulled him back. "We'll finish this on the field, Rhino."

"Can't wait," I said.

After they left, Jamaal, who was watching, said, "Better start checking six, Rhino. You just poured some gas on the fire."

"What fire?"

"Cogan's pissed you're back on the team. And starting at middle linebacker."

"Nobody told me."

"You haven't been around. He thought MIKE was his now. And he says he's going to take you out."

"He knows where I am." I made it sound tougher than I felt. At least it was Cogan's last season. I can deal with that. As long as he didn't make it mine, too.

TEN

AT THE NEXT GROUP, JOSH STOOD UP, LOOKED AROUND as if he owned the group, and said, "So how are we going to respond?"

"Did you have something in mind, Josh?" Ms. L asked.

"We could have been killed," Josh said. "Other kids were injured in our place. We can't wait for the next shooting to get serious, to call for a ban on automatic weapons."

"Was that nationally or just here in Group?" Tyla said. I like her sarcastic edge.

Josh gave her a condescending smile. "It has to start somewhere, Tyla. Why not here, now?"

"Because we're in Woodhaven," Tyla said, "the crossroads of zero and zilch."

"Exactly," Josh said. "This is nowhere. And it didn't even qualify as a mass killing."

"You sound sorry about that," Tyla said.

"Keith was one of us," Josh said. "We need to step up. It's an opportunity to be heard on a critical issue."

Before I thought it through, I said, "You've been trying to be heard since sixth grade. Now you want to take advantage of a tragedy."

Josh's face got red. "Maybe Keith was right; you really are a jock fascist."

I didn't realize that I had stood up and taken a step toward him until I felt a hand clawing through my sweats into my thigh, pulling me back. Strong hand. Tyla's. I looked down into gray eyes. They were intense for gray eyes, a cold ocean.

"That's definitely not fair, Josh," Ms. L said. "But does anyone have a further thought about Josh's suggestion on a gun control protest?"

"It's a good idea," Joy said, "since we're going to get blamed anyway."

"That's wrong," Tyla said. "Keith never said anything about guns or hurting people."

"Look," Josh said, "whether they blame Group isn't as important as the fact that gun violence finally came here. Let's stand up to it."

"Another march?" I asked.

"Why not?" Josh said. "Maybe if we make a stand here in nowhere it might spread to somewhere."

"Good luck," Tyla said. "All those little kids died in Sandy Hook, and nothing happened except a lot of politicians offering their thoughts and prayers."

"So we just give up?" Josh asked. He looked at me. "What do you think, Rhino? About guns."

"Wrong person to ask. I grew up with guns. It's the bad people who shoot the guns you need to lock up."

"You think there should be background checks?" Josh asked.

"Sure." That seemed like a no-brainer. Alison and Dad agreed on that. More or less.

"What about assault rifles?" Josh asked.

"Only if you're expecting a zombie invasion," Tyla said. "You have a plan?"

"To wake people up," Josh said. "A demonstration."

"Great. When?" said Joy so quickly I wondered if they had rehearsed it.

"Homecoming would be a good time."

Disrupt Homecoming, yeah. I was ready for my rematch with Josh right then and there. Good thing Ms. L called time-out then. She actually made the sign with her hands.

I don't remember what else we talked about in that Group. I made sure Josh was off in a corner talking to Ms. L before I started for the door after the bell rang. I didn't trust myself near him.

Out in the hall, when I noticed Tyla next to me, I said, "Thanks. I guess." I think it was the first time I ever directly talked to her.

"You hitting him again wouldn't be good for us, for Group," she said. "We better be together when they come after us."

"They?"

"The school, the town, the cops. They'll need scapegoats for what happened so it doesn't look like their fault. Keith and Ms. L for sure. Then Josh, the rabble-rouser, and the rest of us misfits. All we have is you."

"Me?"

"Yeah, the pale male straight all-American boy. High school hero dates the prom queen, or used to. Maybe you better hook up again." She was talking so fast saliva collected at the corners of her mouth.

"You want to, um, unpack that?"

She took a deep breath. "Sorry, that wasn't very nice." She looked away, then back to me. "I'm freaking out, I guess. Group's been really important to me, keeping me clean. Now it's splitting up into different directions. Everybody's got a plan."

"What's yours?"

"To get my life back?"

I nodded her on. She was slowing down, but still breathing hard. "It feels like my last chance. I don't want to blow it."

"What does that have to do with me?"

"People take you seriously. A football captain. You represent us."

Teachers and kids in the hallway started looking at us. "Later," she said, and hurried away.

I thought, Later is getting very crowded.

ELEVEN

A KIND OF NUMBNESS HAD SETTLED IN THAT WEEK after the shooting. It was much quieter in the halls and the cafeteria. Girls would suddenly break down crying. There were a couple of GoFundMe rallies for kids who were going to have long rehabs. I didn't know any of the wounded kids. Football and debate ate on different sides of the cafeteria. Keith was never mentioned in school. It was like he had disappeared. Andy told me that the next issue of the school paper, which had prepared some big stories about the shooting, including bios of the victims, was canceled.

Only the coaches got louder, trying to crank us up for our next game, an away game against Nearmont, a big rival. Everything was happening so fast. It had been two weeks since I punched Josh, a week since Keith came to school with his gun.

I was dressing with Domi before practice when Jamaal nonchalanted over, pretended to tie his laces, and whispered, "Today's the day. Offense versus defense. If they call the Gronk play, then

Cogan calls 46 Patriots and you get sandwiched between him and Dowling."

"A quarter-ton of prime turd," I said. "Yum."

"No joke, Rhino." Jamaal looked serious.

"Just to keep me out of the Nearmont game? C'mon."

"He wants your ass. He says you think you shit ice cream."

"It's true." I liked Jamaal, but I wasn't going to give anyone the satisfaction of seeing me worried. "Rocky Road, if he wants some."

He slapped my shoulder. "Play the dawg all you want, brother, but you go down, we go with you. Just stay awake."

"Listen to Jamaal," Justin said. "Cogan been mouthing on you nonstop."

"Ever hear of trash talk?" I said.

"He's setting up a hit on you."

I didn't take it seriously. My bad.

For all the coaches' yelling, it was a sluggish practice. Cogan and I took turns running plays at both tight end and middle linebacker, but even when I was opposite Cogan he never came close enough for real contact.

Late in the practice, Dixon and Colligan, as the offensive and defensive coaches, picked guys for a stop-action scrimmage. As if they knew something was up, the rest of the team moved to the sidelines to watch when Cogan went to middle linebacker and I went to tight end. When the quarterback called 87 Gronk, a short pass to me in the flat, Cogan called 46 Pats, in which he and Dowling, the strong safety, trap me.

Domi, who was trailing me on the play, tried to stop it, but Perlick came around and took him out with a vicious block. They had everything planned.

If Jamaal hadn't warned me, I could have gotten hurt. I woke up in time. Cogan is bigger than I am, and Dowling is the hardest hitter on the team. He was going low, right at my knees. I brought my knees up high, sacrificing yardage, and caught him right under the face guard. Thunk! You could hear it. His helmet came off.

Cogan got a piece of me, hit me high with an elbow in the chest. I felt the air whoosh out, but I held on to the ball and staggered another yard before somebody grabbed my ankle. Going down, I scissored my legs, hoping to keep everybody from piling on.

Everybody came up yelling except Dowling, who looked hurt. Justin and Jamaal were shoving Belfer and Cogan, who were laughing at them. They were about to throw punches when the coaches and trainers separated them.

Coach Colligan was screaming into Cogan's face and shaking him by the shoulder pads. I guess 46 Pats was all Cogan's idea.

I looked around for Domi. He was getting up slowly. Perlick was standing nearby, smirking. Domi tapped his helmet in a little two-finger salute. Nice block, Perls, crush you later. Domi was the coolest.

It was quiet and sullen in the locker room. Dowling was off to the hospital with a trainer, maybe with a busted jaw. I hoped not; we needed him. Domi was getting his ribs taped, nothing broken. Cogan shot me lasers from across the room.

Justin was muttering, "Psycho."

"Desperate man does desperate shit," Jamaal said. "He's got no offer. Getting late for him."

"This is no way to get it," Justin said. He poked me. "You all right?"

I nodded and dapped them. Felt a little shook-up. Still sucking air. Trying to think out how to handle this, as a captain. Be hard so long as the coaches allowed the Berserkers to operate as a team inside the team.

Cogan came up with the Berserkers name in his sophomore year, his version of the old-time New York Jets' Sack Exchange, a special unit inside a defensive team. The name was a natural for a team called the Vikings. The Berserkers were the most fearsome Viking warriors, blasted on drugs, wearing smelly bearskins and swinging axes. The name caught on and got some media attention. The coaches liked that, and it fit in with their philosophy that competition within the team kept everybody sharp. I thought it kept everybody disconnected and distrustful, not to mention it seemed to give Cogan permission to be a gang leader in the school.

When it got obvious last year that Cogan and his crew were taking shots at me and bad-mouthing my performance, Dad mentioned it to Coach Dixon. They both drank at the American Legion. Dixon reminded him that Cogan's uncle was the former police chief, and his family was pretty important in town. Dad told me to hang tough.

I have, but it's getting under my skin. Now that I don't have to fantasize about punching Josh, I can fantasize about punching Cogan. Maybe a combination for him, straight right, left hook, right uppercut.

I didn't bother showering, just got out of the locker room as fast as I could, a little surprised that none of the coaches had anything to say to me.

Andy was sitting on his motor scooter alongside my truck when I got to the parking lot. "You okay?"

"With all Coach's bullshit about control, he needs to do something about Cogan."

"Too late," Andy said. "Scumbag runs the team."

"Runs the school," I said. That didn't sound like me. Whiny.

Andy looked around. "I sent you a vid of 46 Pats." He lowered his voice. "It is evidence, man. Plus Coach told me to lose it."

"He was in on it?" I asked.

"I don't think so. But it makes him look bad, shows what a lousy coach he is. It's up to us."

"What is?"

"To get the truth out."

"What are you talking about?" I asked.

"A documentary. Blow the lid off this dumpster fire."

"We need to focus on getting through this year, Andy. Then Cogan will be gone . . ."

"But nothing changes. We need to make a statement. Show where we stand." He was serious.

Everything was hurting. "Sure. I gotta go now."

He pulled a face but nodded. "Later."

Andy took off, spraying gravel. He was in documentary dreamland. Give him a break, Rhino. Dreams are good, especially when everything's going to hell. Andy wants to get out of town as badly as you do.

In the truck, I opened the video attachment from Andy. I had to admit it was a well-executed play. If I hadn't been prepared, I would have been smeared. Maybe say goodbye to at least one knee. But there was no question about what that knee did to Dowling's jaw. I winced watching it. He'll be sipping his steak through a straw. He deserved it. They'll want payback.

TWELVE

I DIDN'T SHOW THE VID TO ANYONE. I DOWNLOADED IT to my computer, backed it up on the encrypted external drive where I keep this journal and a few other writings, then deleted it from my phone and computer. I felt like an electronic spy.

I soaked in a hot bathtub. Ice might have been better, but I needed comfort. The red overload button was flashing in my brain. Too much going on—the shooting, football, Group, Tyla, Cogan, the history paper. I needed to clear space. I'd been having trouble getting to sleep, and I'd wake up early with a boulder on my chest.

Tyla? Did I say Tyla? Why is she on that list?

I was reading for the history paper when Josh called. I didn't recognize the number, and I almost let it go as spam. But I was looking for a reason to take a break, even if I had to risk talking to somebody about extending my auto warranty.

"Ron?"

"Yeah."

"It's Josh. Josh Kremens." The voice didn't seem so sure of itself. "Can we talk?"

"That's what we're doing."

"I mean like in person."

"About what?"

There was a long pause. "We need to get together, to make a plan."

I laughed. "Yeah, right. How we'll march together at Homecoming?"

"Serious stuff is dropping, man, we need to deal with it. It's why I want to talk." He made it sound urgent.

"Why me?"

"I trust you."

I thought about that. Too weird. But I knew I was trustworthy. In some way, I thought he was, too. Or at least predictable. "Where?"

"Behind the Walmart?"

"When?"

"Now."

"Gimme ten," I said.

I slipped out of the house. I didn't want to tell anyone where I was going, and I didn't want to lie. It was all feeling too strange to explain.

I thought Josh would be driving a fancier car, a Beamer M maybe or a Camaro ZL1, but he pulled up in a dusty Toyota Camry. He jumped out, looked around nervously, and climbed into the passenger seat of my truck. It's easy to spot with the Vikings logo on the doors. And rust everywhere else.

"Thanks for coming," he said.

"So what's this about?"

"They're going to fire Ms. Lamusciano, blame the shooting on her and Group."

"Who is?"

"The town, the school board. The cops. Dr. Mullins."

He looked grim and maybe scared. I tried to get my head around what he was saying. "How do you know all this?"

"My dad. Point is, if what happened can be blamed on this one bad program, bad psychologist, bad kid, the town is off the hook and there's no big fallout, no gun control fuss. No progress."

"And you have a plan."

He ignored my cold tone. "We can't let it get buried. Until it happens again. We need to stand up and ask how Keith Korn got an AR-15 and got so close to a mass killing, and then we need to take the next step and make the town ban those assault weapons."

"Can a town do that?"

"It can make a statement, at least. Show where we stand."

Sounded like Andy. Were they talking? "Good luck."

"I'm serious. We need you."

"You know it's not my thing. We own guns. I shoot them. My dad's a cop."

"That's why we need you. They can't just brush you off as another left-wing puke. And it's not just about guns. It's about this town always sweeping everything under the rug, the bullies taking over." He sounded like he was raving.

"Look, I'm just a football player . . ."

"That's the point. Keith was coming to kill you."

"Why?"

"He said he thought jocks were the problem, and you were put in Group to spy on him."

"How do you know this?"

"Between us?"

"Yeah."

"My dad got a look at some of the state police and ATF interviews, and their psychiatrist's notes. Your coming into Group set him off."

"Okay, so we got one kid with issues who gets an assault rifle, which sounds like a mental health problem to me, and a bunch of bullies on the football team, that happens, and a town that doesn't want a bad image, what's new? And a baby politician marching around trying to make a name for himself as some kind of hero . . ."

"That's what you think of me?" Josh looked hurt.

"That's what I think." I looked hard at him. It was my dare-you-to-take-a-swing look. I was fed up.

He sank into himself, almost collapsed like I punched him again. "That's not it at all. I thought you were getting it." There was a pleading in his voice I'd never heard before. "Woodhaven's coming apart. The bullies, the guns, the censorship. You heard about the school paper? Cogan and Keith are symptoms of a terrible disease."

"And you're Dr. Kremens with the cure. Demonstrations."

He blinked, as if I'd slapped him, but he kept coming. "We need to force people to wake up, face the issues, talk about them, guns, climate change, sexual harassment, inequality. Our generation is going to have to deal with this stuff, the sooner the better." He looked at his phone. "I got to get back before my dad does. I'm grounded. You'll think about this, doing something with us?"

He was out of the truck hurrying back to his car before I could come up with an answer.

On my way out of the Walmart lot, I thought somebody honked at me, but my mind was somewhere else. What does that mean,

You'll think about this, doing something with us? Like, make it my problem, too? Was it my problem? Is everything my problem?

I killed the headlights before I pulled into the driveway and went around the back. My phone burped with a text. I shut it off. I planned on sneaking up to my room, avoiding anybody who might be downstairs. But Butkus sniffed me out and met me at the back door, so I took him for a walk. He'd be my alibi if anybody asked where I'd been. Why should I have to lie? Why is everything beginning to feel like a crime series?

Maybe because it was turning into a crime series. Keith coming after me as his bully? He was insane. Cogan targeting my knees? There's a real bully. We never like to think another baller could bully us even though it happens all the time. Intimidation is part of the game. So maybe Keith is right about jocks.

So, you can't trust a teammate, and your enemy asks you to trust him. Is Cogan really my teammate? Is Josh my enemy? Is this ambiguity?

If I ended up doing something with Josh, it would all be too bizarre. Even for whatever Andy is cooking up and wants to drag me into.

Mom and Livy were at the dining room table working on homework when I got back with Butkus.

"Where've you been?" Mom asked.

"Walking the dog."

"You've never walked him so much," Mom said. There was a question in her voice that asked, *What's going on?*

"They have a lot to talk about," Livy said. "Like books."

Mom snorted but let it go. Thanks, kid. I owe you one. I headed upstairs.

THIRTEEN

THE BUS RIDE TO NEARMONT WAS UNUSUALLY QUIET
except for occasional bursts of cheering from the Berserkers, who sat
up front, behind the coaches. The cheering sounded forced. Nobody
was really up for the game. Some of the guys were talking about the
49ers' quarterback Colin Kaepernick kneeling during the national
anthem before NFL games to protest racism and police brutality.
He'd only done it for a couple of games, but lots of people were
talking about it, especially on TV. It sounded like Jamaal and Justin
wanted to kneel, but most of the others were opposed, especially the
Berserkers.

I wanted to break up any divisive talk before a game, so I said, "I
hear Nearmont's got a quarterback this year."

"Hella arm," somebody said, "but can't move. Hides in the
pocket."

"We'll get him."

Nice. For the rest of the ride we talked about the game.

I pulled Jamaal into a corner of the Nearmont visitors' locker room. "Not today."

He knew what I was talking about. "You going to tell me when?" It was like a dare.

"Coach'll kick you off the team."

"Not so long as he needs an all-county runner."

"Don't count on that. Lots of political pressure." I put my hand on his arm.

He pulled it away.

The Nearmont band played the national anthem, and I checked the line of players. Jamaal looked jittery, shifting from foot to foot, but at least he was standing. I didn't want to have to deal with a kneeling situation my first game as a captain.

I felt the usual pre-kickoff ice ball, which was a good sign, and then the ball was in the air and everything was back to normal. What's normal? Football.

Nearmont brought the ball up to its thirty-five-yard line.

"Rhino!" Coach Colligan was slapping my helmet. "MIKE sticks with Bearcub first couple downs; remember number twelve's strictly a pocket passer."

I led the defense out and took my position as middle linebacker, comfortable but still surprised I got it back after missing the first game. Cogan didn't look at me. The huddle seemed sloppy.

"C'mon, c'mon, tighten it," I yelled. "Bearcub." As the defense closed around me, I noticed Cogan smirking at me.

Bearcub is a straight three-man pass rush to disrupt the quarterback as our safeties and corners drop back, looking to intercept. If we kept up the pressure, we could bottle up number 12. The team practiced that all week.

Lining up, the Nearmont center yelled, "Watch 53 MIKE, Bear-cub," alerting his linemen to focus on me and revealing our play. How did he know?

On the line of scrimmage, I changed the play to "Hercules," a five-man blitz.

It should have worked. I felt jacked, a missile headed for a sack, but a two-man blitz is a suicide mission and that's what it turned out to be, just me and Justin banging against the U-shaped pocket around number 12. Cogan and his pals, Belfer and Perlick, were two steps behind us, laughing. They had bailed out of the play, leaving Justin and me to get our butts kicked.

We were blocked hard, and number 12 got his pass off, a long one to a guy who went all the way for a touchdown. On the first play of the game! He wasn't that fast, but our secondary had come in to support Hercules and the receiver went fifty-five yards after the catch. He had just enough energy to spike the ball in the end zone, then grab his kneecaps and bend over, gasping. His team jumped all over him. The coaches ran out to hug him. They should have been hugging the rat who gave our play away. Cogan? Just to make me look bad? Am I getting into conspiracy theory here?

I was yelling at Cogan as I walked to the sidelines with Justin. Words you wouldn't like, Ms. L.

Justin was steaming, too. "What do you want to do?"

"I don't know." I really didn't. Fighting Cogan here and now sounded good, but it wasn't something a football captain should do. We had no proof. Trying to suck it up and get through the game probably wouldn't work either, but it was all I could think of.

"Just play the game," I said to Justin. "Keep your eyes open."

Coach Colligan grabbed me as I came off the field. "What

happened? What did you call?"

"Ask Cogan." I shook him off and walked away.

I kept walking around to the back of the grandstand. Needed to think. I guess my head was down because I walked right into Dad. He tries to make all my games. This time I was glad to see him.

"What happened?" He grabbed my arms.

They felt weak. "I called a five-man blitz, and Cogan and his two buddies stayed back."

Dad cursed. "They should be thrown off the team."

"I don't know what to do." I felt like a little kid.

"You tell Colligan?"

"No."

"Okay. Then you just suck it up and play the game. Go back." Cool Dad was gone.

"I can't."

"You have to. You can't let them win." His face was red and clenched. "You can't walk away. You have to stay and fight. Like Ali."

Where did that come from? "Like Ali?"

"Whatever the bastards threw at him, he took it and kept going, did it his way until he won."

He was angry, but I was numb. "What if Cogan does it again?"

"He won't. Colligan's a wuss; he won't put you back at middle linebacker once he figures out what happened, because he's afraid of Cogan. Just get through the game. Don't let them think they got to you."

He punched my arm and pushed me back to the sideline. Nearmont made the extra point and we set up to receive. Jamaal brought it up to our forty. Dixon sent a grinning Cogan in at tight end. I stayed on the bench. Was I being punished for something?

I was in and out of the game. I don't remember much of it, but I got through. Just sucked it up. Muscle memory. I only played offense. Hit, got hit, blocked. Don't ask me what happened. Watch Andy's video, if you care. Nearmont won by twenty. We were 0–2.

I was in no mood, but I went to the Vikings Against Cancer party in the hospital lobby as I promised Maddie. She was waiting for me at the door. Big smile and a hug. Some girls cheered. I wondered what that was all about. Maddie went off to organize some more photo ops, and I spotted Tyla handing out little swag bags with brochures and Woodhaven caps. I went over.

"Hey. What are you doing here?"

"Community service. Hey, listen, I'm sorry about dumping on you the other day, I just . . ."

Suddenly, Maddie had an arm linked in mine and was pulling me away. "Need him for a photo op." When we were a few feet away, she said, "A new friend?"

"From Group."

"No wonder you like it so much."

I ignored it. I wasn't in a crime series after all. I was in a teen romance. More dangerous.

Andy appeared. I remembered he was shooting video for the cancer campaign. He gestured to us. "A little closer, please," he said, shooting.

After Maddie released me, I drifted around the lobby, gabbing with guys on the team and some teachers who wanted to talk football, waiting for a good time to slip out.

Mr. Biedermann walked up. "I think it's a good idea," he said.

"What?"

"Combining forces. As long as you really contribute, write some of the documentary."

It took me a minute to realize Andy must have gone ahead and pitched his blowing-the-lid doc and included me. Hey, everybody's got a plan for me. I was too tired to think straight anyway. "Sure," I said.

Another teacher pulled him away. I looked for Tyla, but she must have split. Me too.

Back home I found the Percocet and got a beer and went to bed.

FOURTEEN

I WOKE UP TO LIVY POUNDING ON MY DOOR. "BREAK-fast," she yelled. The thought made me nauseous.

I managed a weak "Beat it."

"Twenty minutes we leave for church."

I heard Dad talking to her, then arguing with Mom. He came into my room. I buried my face in my pillow. I could feel his breath in my ear. "Sleep it off, Ronnie, we'll be out most of the day." He squeezed my shoulder. "Just a bad game. Get past it."

I hope he heard me mumble "Thanks."

Around noon, I hauled out of bed. Showered forever and drank gallons of coffee. Buttered toast. I walked Butkus, stretched, sprinted a few minutes on the stationary bike, stretched, lifted light weights. Eggs and more toast. More coffee. Began to come to life.

The phone kept chiming, buzzing, ringing, burping. Too foggy to remember what each meant. I kept checking for Alison or Ms. L, the only people I wanted to talk to. I had Ms. L's cell number, she'd given it to everybody in Group, but what would I say? I'm feeling depressed, under attack, like nobody has my back? Please help me?

Captains don't whine.

I pulled on clean jeans and a shirt that wasn't too wrinkled and a jacket without any logos—she hated logos—and got into the truck and headed west.

I sent two texts, one to Andy that read **Staying over** and one to Mom saying, **Staying over Andy's.** He'd know to cover for me, and she never checked because I was such a straight arrow. I felt a guilty twinge.

I drove for five hours, audio blasting, singing along when it was country. I like most music—*Machinery* is only for workouts— especially rap, cool jazz, and Beethoven and Mahler symphonies, which Alison turned me on to.

I got to her campus around dinnertime and found her dorm. Sophomore year she had scored a first-floor single close to the classroom buildings and the cafeteria, a nice room she had turned into a hermit's cave, overflowing with books and computer gear and speakers. She sent me pictures once. She didn't go out much.

When I walked into the dorm, a campus security guard, an old guy with a giant flashlight, came out of the shadows of the lobby. "Can I help you?"

"Yes, thank you," I said cheerfully, like Dad taught me, my hands in sight. My size makes cop types nervous. I can't imagine being Black, but I've seen cops white-knuckle their Tasers when they don't know me. "I'm looking for Alison Rhinehart."

He took his time, looking me over. Finally, he said, "She doesn't live here," as if he were glad.

"It's her school address."

"The big girl?" He smirked at me.

"Did she move?"

"I don't give out information on residents. Better go to the office."

"Where's that?"

"It's closed now." The old coot seemed glad about that, too.

"Maybe I can just wait and ask someone who might know."

"Then you'd be trespassing." He slapped the flashlight against an open palm.

I gave myself a few seconds of fantasizing picking him up and throwing him across the lobby before I remembered that Dad did this kind of job these days. I flashed him a phony Rhino smile. "I understand, sir. I'm her brother. The family is trying to reach her."

He thought about that for a while. "Come back tomorrow. The office opens at nine."

"Thank you, sir."

I left without looking back and walked past my truck and into the shadows thrown by tall trees. I waited until he had gone back to his hidey-hole in the lobby then came halfway back.

Students were coming out of the cafeteria. The first girl who looked at me without fear got the Rhino smile. "Excuse me, do you know Alison Rhinehart?"

That drew a blank, but the next one nodded. "The big girl? She moved out."

"You know where she is?"

She turned to her friend, who shook her head, then started asking other kids until one said, "I think she's at that place for old dogs." She pointed into the darkness. "It's off Emerson Road, maybe five miles?"

I found a website for a senior dog shelter and followed directions to Emerson. After three miles I drove slowly until I saw the sign at the end of a dirt road: THE SENIOR DOG HAVEN. A quarter mile up the road the barking began, and then dogs came up to the wire fence, some of them running, some of them shambling along. I pulled up near an old house.

There was a flashlight in my eyes, then a familiar voice. "What are you doing here?"

"Hello to you, too."

"They send you?"

"They don't know where I am." I took a deep breath. "I don't know where I am either."

I could hear her breathing, raspier than I remembered. "C'mon."

I followed the flashlight beam over a gravel path that led alongside the fence. Dogs wandered over to bark and sniff. Alison opened a door, then gestured me into a small front room with a huge couch, a TV, books everywhere. When she turned to face me in the light, she seemed bigger than she was the last time I'd seen her, more than a year ago.

"Well, you're still growing, too," she said.

Then we both laughed, and she pulled me into a hug.

"You hungry?"

"Thirsty."

I let her push me into the couch. She left and came back with flavored seltzer and pretzel chips.

"You live here?"

"I'm managing the place."

"You dropped out?"

"You came up to ask me this?"

"Answer your email I wouldn't have to."

"Maybe I wanted you to come. So what's up, pup? You look like roadkill."

"Thanks."

"You okay?"

"Not really," I said.

"Tell me about it. I've got time and room."

I began to relax. Alison was like that, always thorny to start, then ready to help. I was glad to be there.

"I'm having trouble sorting things out."

"Welcome to the club. That shooting was a big deal, even if nobody got killed."

"Turns out he was coming to kill me. There was a last-minute room change."

"Lucky for you."

"There's other stuff."

"Always is. Let's get some sleep, the dogs get fed early. We'll have time to talk."

I got settled in a room upstairs. It was small and smelled musty, the bed was not much more than a cot and dogs were barking, but the minute my head hit the stony little pillow, the world went away.

FIFTEEN

HARD SUNLIGHT WOKE ME UP. THROUGH THE DUSTY window, I watched Alison moving through the pack, petting and scratching and talking to maybe thirty old dogs, filling their food and water bowls, accepting their licks and rubs like a queen with her subjects. She looked happy.

They called her the big girl. People couldn't look past that. As a kid she was always going on diets, to shrinks, was even sent away to a fat camp. Dad thought she lacked willpower, that she needed to try harder. He fat-shamed her, even in public. Mom thought it was bad genes, maybe from Dad's side of the family where they drank too much. I wondered if Mom and Dad made it into more of a problem than it had to be and drove Alison away. What about all those obese NFL linemen? They looked happy and healthy. I never got to talk about that with anybody. What do you think, Ms. L?

I heard Alison coming back into the house, so I dressed and went downstairs. She'd started making breakfast.

"Those dogs love you," I said.

"I feed them." She broke six eggs into a bowl, whipped them, and poured them into a hot pan. She dropped four slices of bread into the toaster. "Coffee?"

"You serious?"

She ate slowly, small bites. Sipped her coffee.

She smiled. "So, what's the story, morning glory?" The old line relaxed me.

I told her most everything, from punching Josh Kremens to Group and Ms. Lamusciano, the journal, the shooting, Cogan on my ass, and Josh wanting us to get together for a gun control campaign. I even mentioned Tyla. I told her everything I could think of except ripping the Post-it off the wall outside the conference room. Just thinking about it made my throat close. She looked at me and nodded the whole time, big warm brown eyes drinking everything in. I felt safe. I really did miss her. I thought about times coming home after getting bullied at peewee and she made me feel better. I never knew she was hurting, too.

She said, "So where was Sergeant in all this?"

"Dad stood up to Mr. Kremens and the school . . ."

"He was trying to take control, as usual."

"He was trying to keep me from getting expelled . . ."

"From getting kicked off the team."

"Well, yeah, but that was still support. Told me to keep my eyes on the prize, not to walk away. He said, You have to stay and fight for what you believe in."

Her eyes narrowed at that. "He actually said that? To stay and fight for what you believe in?"

"Yeah. Like Ali. Why?"

"I think it still bugs him that he didn't push back harder when the state police didn't support him right away."

"I never knew the full story, just that he got blamed for some kind of car crash that wasn't his fault."

"It was and it wasn't. He chased a suspect into a populated area, which you're not supposed to do, and the guy crashed into some citizen's car and injured her. She was Black. So was the suspect. Big fuss. Dad was eventually cleared, but the state police put him on some kind of desk duty, let him hang in the wind for months. He got mad and quit. He blamed it all on the troopers rolling over for Black Lives Matter and liberals. You must have heard that."

"He and Gramps think Trump's going to fix all that."

"Thank the goddess he won't have the chance. Two months to the election and then you'll never hear of the Donald again. How's Gramps doing?"

I remembered the fights they had. "Like you care."

She gave me a strange look. "He's my grandfather. Even if his brain is on another planet. Anything else new?"

I told her about the paper for Mr. Biedermann turning into a documentary with Andy and she seemed interested. "He was the only teacher I liked. So, what about this Ms. L?"

"She means well."

"All those social worker shrinks mean well, but they don't always know how to help you. You get anything out of Group?"

"It feels like a waste of time."

"Give it a chance. What about this Josh dude?"

"Don't really trust him."

"Why?"

"He's trying to take over."

"Somebody needs to. Town should ban assault rifles. And you kids should lead the way, since you're the ones most likely to get killed." Alison can make sense like that. She said, "So that's the headlines. What about you? How's your love life?"

"Maddie and I broke up."

She nodded like she wasn't surprised. "Barbie and Ken. Nice girl but a little shallow for you. Seeing anybody else?"

"No." I had a mental flash of Tyla. "Time to drill down on football."

"Hope you're writing everything down in your journal. Great way to think things through."

"You keep one?"

"Got a pile of them."

"What are you writing about these days?"

She cocked an eyebrow. "Isn't it time you headed back? Don't you have practice? Group?"

Talk about deflecting. "Hey, Allie, don't shut me out. I care about you. And I trust you. Why do you think I'm here?"

Were Alison's eyes wet? "I know, Ronnie. I'm glad you're here."

"The dogs need you," I said. "It's a good thing. But what about you?"

"I don't have to think about that for now, just take care of them. They're happy, the shelter people are happy. I've set up a website for them, going to start blogging for fosters and adoptions . . ." She shrugged.

"How long's that going to last?" I asked.

"How long's football going to last?"

"Football's a means to an end, a getaway, college."

"Maybe. If you don't get hurt or cut. But you're also losing yourself in football, you don't have to deal with anything else in your life as long as you stay buried in the game. And everyone else cuts you slack."

I felt uncomfortable thinking about football that way. I love the game, and I wanted to believe it would give me an escape from Woodhaven, not an escape from real life.

I remembered something a coach had once said, and I repeated it. "Football is realer than life."

Alison laughed through her nose. "That's the kind of crap only a coach would say." She looked at her watch. "Speaking of which. Time for poop patrol."

I stood up. My hammies complained. We'd been talking a long time. "Give you a hand?"

"Thanks, but no thanks. You've got a long drive. And a lot of *real* shit waiting for you."

"Maybe I'll just keep burying myself in it."

I guess the sarcasm didn't come through because Alison nodded and said, "Think about it, Ronnie. Think about who you want to be. You have a chance to be someone special. You don't have to be Rhino. Or just Rhino."

I kind of knew what she meant, at least enough not to want to ask her to explain more and have to deal with it right now.

She made me ham-and-cheese sandwiches and packed them in a bag with a couple of bottles of water, fruit, and cookies. She walked me out to the truck.

"What should I say to them?" I asked.

"That I'm okay, as if they cared."

"If I call, will you pick up?"

"I might." She gave me a long hug. "You were always my favorite brother."

"I'd like to come back. Maybe stay awhile, help out."

"Maybe." I could see her eyes getting wet again before she turned away and headed to the dogs.

The trip back went fast. I thought about Alison. The dogs didn't care what she looked like as long as she fed them and loved them. But the rest of the world . . .

I was headed back to the rest of the world.

SIXTEEN

IT'S BEEN MORE THAN THREE WEEKS SINCE THE SHOOT-
ing, and the conference room is still a shrine of flowers, notes,
photos. The Group was still meeting down in the old day care room.
Joy, Marco, and Tyla were staring at different corners of the ceiling
when I walked in late. Ms. L was listening to Josh, who for once was
talking softly.

"We could meet somewhere else, outside school," he was saying,
"and you could call in, Skype, speakerphone, whatever."

"I can't participate at all," Ms. L said. Her face was pale and her
eyes red-rimmed. "They were very specific."

"They won't know," Josh said. He looked around the room.
"Agreed?"

Everybody nodded, even Marco. That surprised me.

"What's up?" I asked.

"Ms. L has been fired," Joy said.

"They're canceling Group," Josh said. "It's part of blaming us for
Keith."

"Blaming me," Ms. L said quickly. "You guys had nothing to do with what happened."

I felt a sharp pang in my gut. I certainly had something to do with what happened.

"What about us?" Joy asked. "In lieu of detention?"

"You'll have the chance to see counselors individually," Ms. L said. "That and more community service should satisfy the court."

"We were getting somewhere here," Joy said. "We were getting support from each other."

"Maybe Josh is right," I said. "We could meet on our own somewhere." I liked the way that sounded. Captain-ish.

"They want to sweep it all under the table, like it never happened," Josh said.

"Josh is right," Marco said. We looked at him. I couldn't remember hearing him speak in Group before. He had a high voice. "The cops for sure. I hear them talking."

"More reason for us to stick together," Tyla said.

We talked for a while. The word had come down from Dr. Mullins, who was back at work a couple days a week. Group canceled, Ms. L sent to another school district, the kids in Group, in the Debate Club, and anyone with traumatic distress would be assigned psych counselors who would come to Woodhaven. End of story. Moving on.

"Who wants to start with strangers?" Joy said. "We're like family here."

"Which family," Tyla said, "the Kardashians, the Munsters?"

We all laughed, including Marco. If Group gets to that hooded blob, something is happening. I felt good about that. But why? I had football if I needed another family.

"We can keep the spirit of Group alive by staying in touch with each other and writing in our journals," Ms. L said. She started crying. Joy hugged her.

"We can do more than that," Josh said. "Mr. Biedermann's church has a room he said we can use. I've got some new members lined up."

"I'd be careful," Ms. L said. "Keep it small, the original group for a while. The administration really wants to shut this down."

"This isn't going to be a political organization," I said.

"Everything's political," Josh said. "We need to go beyond Group if we want to get anything done."

"Done like what?" I asked. "Demonstrate at football games?"

Ms. L made her time-out sign. "Whatever you guys do, it has to be together."

"Count me in," Marco said. He opened his arms. Ms. L hugged him and then Tyla and Joy made it a group hug. Josh and I looked at each other, then went over and sort of patted their backs.

The hug broke up at a knocking on the door. The vice principal walked in.

"Ms. Lamusciano? Dr. Mullins would like to see you in her office. Right away." He waited while Ms. L scooped up her purse, briefcase, and thermos, waved goodbye, and left the room.

"School day's over," said the vice principal. "Unless you have practice, Rhino."

"I do."

"Better go." He glared me out of the room and closed the door behind me. Through the glass, I could see him jawing at Josh while the others stared at them. I would have liked to hear what was going on. I thought I should be in there with them. My friends.

Cogan trotted over when I jogged onto the field. "Where were you yesterday . . . Captain?"

"Ask your mother."

"I just wanted to thank you, Rhino. I'm starting against Ridge-field Park."

I was about to say *Try not to screw up,* but I managed to swallow it back. Be cool. Don't let them bait you, pull you into traps. I walked away.

Coach Dixon grabbed my face mask. "Where were you yesterday?"

"Family," I mumbled, sorry I even went that far.

"Then you call. We've got a game on Saturday. You know how important Monday practice is. That's why Cogan is starting."

I nodded, kept my eyes down. *I don't really care, Coach. Got other things on my mind right now.*

It took concentration to keep focused on practice even though the coaches hadn't installed anything new yesterday and it wasn't hard to run through the old plays. My head just wasn't there. Cogan was at middle linebacker and tight end; I was outside linebacker and stuck into different slots on the offensive line depending on whether we were practicing pass or rushing plays. It was supposed to be a half-speed workout, no hard hitting, but I got a few unnecessary knees and kicks from the Berserkers. I didn't react.

But I needed to leave before I did react. I could feel something hot bubbling up. I was the first one out of the locker room, without showering. Andy caught up to me in the parking lot.

"You okay?"

"I'm fine." I didn't realize how sharply I snapped at him until he raised his hands and took a step back.

"Hey, just asking."

"Sorry, Andy."

"Yeah, well . . ." He looked around. "Cogan and his shitheads are spreading stuff about you and Josh Kremens."

"What about?"

"Somebody spotted you guys in the Walmart parking lot. Said you were making out."

"We're queer?" It made me laugh.

"They're after you, Ron. We got to do something."

"Just get through the season."

"It's more than football. It's this school. This town."

"Tell me about it."

"We need to talk about what we're doing for Mr. Biedermann."

"Thanks for running it past me."

"Thought you would like it, too. An Andiron Production."

"What would I do? Mr. Biedermann has me into the whole historical football-slavery thing."

"It could start there, I guess, but we would focus on Woodhaven now, football as king, the Berserkers, Keith Korn, how screwed up everything is."

"I'll think about it." I kind of snapped it.

"You do that." He walked away in a huff.

I felt sorry and started to call him back, but the words got stuck in a dry throat. Everybody's got an attitude these days.

SEVENTEEN

AT DINNER, I GAVE A REPORT ON ALISON, MOSTLY ABOUT how great she was with dogs. Mom and Livy hung on every word. Dad's facial expressions tried to indicate that he wasn't interested, but his tense body language gave him away.

Mom said, "Is she still as, um, big?"

Why is it always back to that? I said, "She seems happy."

"Did you think we'd try to stop you from going?" Dad asked. "Saying you were staying at Andy's."

"Last-minute decision, change of plans." I knew that made no sense and that everybody knew it was a lie, but nobody challenged it. I wondered if they had secretly wanted me to go visit her, just not tell them beforehand. They cared, too.

Dad left the table.

"It's not her fault," Livy said. "We were studying obesity in Health . . ."

"It's complicated," Mom said, shutting her off. "Did she officially drop out?"

"I think so," I said. "She's doing really well at her job, she's . . ."

"What a waste," Mom said. She had to blow her nose and wipe her eyes. "She was so smart."

"Still is," I said. "We had good conversations."

"What did she say about Dad and me?"

"She kept calling him Sergeant."

Mom nodded. "They were so close when she was little; she was the apple of Dad's eye. I don't know what happened."

Like he'd caught a vibe, Dad walked back into the dining room. He was holding a glass of colorless fluid, probably not water. That was never a good sign.

"Can we talk about something else?"

"What?" Mom asked.

"I got a call from Kremens," he said.

I perked up. This wasn't a good sign either. "What's he want?"

"To meet with me."

"About what?" I asked.

"That's what I'd like to know," Dad said. "You boys up to something?"

"Like what?"

Dad slammed his hand on the table. "That's not answering my question. What's going on with Group?"

"It got canceled."

"That's what he said. Good. You can concentrate on ball. Anything else going on?"

"Why'd you go up?" Mom asked, redirecting the conversation.

"I was worried about her, she never answered anything," I said. Not the whole truth. I was worried about myself, too.

Dad looked at me and his face sagged from angry to sad. Then he nodded and walked out again.

Mom waited until he couldn't hear us. "He cares more than you think."

"He should," I said. "I think she feels rejected. He could reach out more." Livy gave me a strange look. I realized I never talked like this. Is this from Group?

"It's hard for him to deal with feelings," Mom said. This was more sharing than I'd expect from her.

"We have to support each other," I said.

Now Mom gave me that strange look.

"I'll clean up," I said.

Mom and Livy looked grateful to go upstairs. I don't mind loading the dishwasher and scrubbing pots and wiping the table and counters. Reminds me of water play when I was a kid. And you get results. Inside an hour you've solved problems, erased a mess. You've scored and won.

Upstairs, I brought the latest draft of the history paper up on the screen. I was still struggling to tie up racism, football, athletes' rights, and Muhammad Ali in one essay, but I was getting closer. That is, when I wasn't getting distracted by other interesting stuff. I hadn't known that Woody Strode, a Black actor I liked in a great western called *The Professionals,* had been a college football star before becoming one of the first Black players in the NFL in 1946. That was only a year before Jackie Robinson arrived in major league baseball. Woody and Jackie were football teammates at UCLA. I started thinking about segregation in sports. I never read that much about it. Was that something we weren't supposed to know about? Why? And who was afraid of the truth coming out?

My head started buzzing just thinking about it. But some part of me felt a little sorry to give up my paper to do the doc with Andy. This was interesting stuff. And I wondered if there was a connection between this history and what was happening in school, between my essay and Andy's doc. I was thinking about calling him to apologize when the phone rang. Thinking it might be him, I answered before checking caller ID.

"Is everything all right? You ditched school." It was Madison, breathless.

"I went up to see Alison."

"That's wonderful. How'd it go?"

There was real concern in her voice. "It was pretty good, I think. We both talked and well . . ." I trailed off. I didn't feel like spilling over the phone.

"You don't have to tell me everything right now. I'm really glad for you, Ronnie. I know you love each other and need each other's support." She took a little breath as if she was gathering strength. "I heard they canceled Group. Are you okay with that?"

"It is what it is. They want to make Ms. Lamusciano the scapegoat."

"Some people think she should have seen the red flags."

"Then what?"

"I don't know. Tell the principal, call the police, make sure he didn't have guns."

"I don't think that's so easy."

"I'm sure you're right." She took another energizing breath. "Thanks for coming to Vikings Against Cancer. Pictures came out great."

"Pictures?" Then I remembered the hug.

"Phoebe is having a party Saturday. Sort of a rally for the kids who got hurt."

I wanted to remind her we were broken up, but thinking about the hug reminded me of talking to Tyla that night. Phoebe's party sounded like another possible community service gig for Tyla. "I should be back from the game in time. Sounds good."

"That's great. See ya." It seemed like she got off the line before I could think about it and change my mind. She wants to get back together. I have to be careful I don't string her along.

Dad didn't have much to say when he came back from meeting Mr. Kremens other than he wasn't such a bad guy. They were going to work together to make sure any police records on me and Josh would be deleted. I could tell there was more, but Dad is always good at keeping secrets. He didn't mention anything about Keith targeting me.

Andy didn't bring up the rumors about me and Josh again, but I noticed that kids from the Rainbow Alliance weren't going out of their way to avoid me in the halls like they usually did with football players, who would throw a shoulder or elbow their way. I never did, but I guess they just saw the varsity jacket not the face. I thought it was kind of funny, although I did wonder if a rumor I was gay would turn off a Division I coach. I heard NFL coaches were asking very personal questions at the combines. And there were still no openly gay pro players.

On Friday, Mr. Biedermann snagged me after history.

"I hear you and Josh are going to keep Group going."

"We'll try. At your church. You going to come by?"

"We'll see. Have a good game."

I didn't. Cogan made sure of that.

I guess I should empathize with his desperation, seven months from graduation without serious Division I attention. But that doesn't buy you permission to be a psycho.

Okay, so Cogan wanted a shot at looking good, but he also wanted a chance to get revenge for his buddy Dowling, whose broken jaw was still wired. Coach gave him both chances by letting him start at MIKE and tight end. I wasn't happy about it, but it was the least of my problems. I'd have my chance to shine all next season. The letters and emails I'd gotten from college coaches had tapered off because of the season we were having, but I knew a few wins would change that. I just needed to make it to next season. Cogan would be gone. Weren't the coaches interested in keeping me healthy?

Ridgefield Park was a good team. They played tight ball. They dominated the first half, keeping possession, and our defense struggled to hold them to two field goals. We were losing 6–0 deep in the third quarter on our thirty-yard line when Cogan called a play for me to shoot a gap and hit the quarterback from the blind side. Belfer, at tackle, was supposed to clear me some space between a monster end and an all-state tackle, the blind side. It never occurred to me Cogan would set me up in another trap. My naive bad.

Belfer barely tried to make it look legit. He fell before anyone touched him. I juked around the monster guard, but the left tackle nailed me hard. My head slammed into the ground. There was a one-second lights out. Maybe two.

Domi helped me up. I shrugged him off and staggered away to line up with the Ridgefield Park team. Cogan and Belfer were laughing as two trainers hurried out to lead me off the field.

Ridgefield Park had a state-of-the-art trainer's room. I thought I was in an ER. I saw Dad and a doctor peering over another doctor's shoulders as she pointed a little flashlight in my eyes. Then I was in an ambulance.

After all the media attention lately to NFL concussions, I was pretty sure I had one. I'd had them before, but like most football players I managed to hide them for a few days until my head cleared. This one felt different right away, bad headache, nausea, wobbly. Bright lights hurt my eyes.

There were some more tests in the hospital. I went on a concussion protocol. I had to stay overnight for observation. Miss the party. Maddie was very understanding. Why did that make me feel grateful and annoyed at the same time? Rhino needs his head examined.

EIGHTEEN

I SPENT SUNDAY AND MONDAY IN MY BEDROOM, LIGHTS off, blinds down. Mom and Livy programmed yacht rock on Spotify, and even that soft, cheesy music sounded loud. I kept my eyes closed in the darkness, trying to shut out my thoughts along with the light. Thoughts hurt, too. Football isn't my safe place anymore. It wasn't about getting hurt. I'd been hurt plenty: sprains, lacerations, pulled muscles, a broken wrist, you name it, unreported concussions. It was part of the game. But I'd never felt under attack from inside before. From my own team. It hurt.

Dad told me we'd won the game, 7–6. Jamaal broke loose for a sixty-yard touchdown run in the fourth quarter. He thought it would make me feel better, but it didn't do anything at all. We were 1–2 now, still in a hole. I felt deeper in a hole. Dad said if we won Homecoming, we'd be 2–2, still have a chance to salvage a winning season, maybe even make a run at conference. I didn't care. It didn't matter. Nothing mattered under the blanket of silence and darkness.

I wonder if this is what depression feels like, a darkness even darker than a room with drawn blinds and eyes closed. I stayed in bed into a third day.

I don't know if I was actually asleep or just drifting to some Taylor Swift soft rock Livy had programmed when Rhino's Run flickered in my brain. The ball bounced off my shoelaces into my arms. I bobbled it as I started to run downfield, Tyla alongside, holding out her arms. I let the ball float into her hands. She threw it back to me. I was reaching for it.

"Ronnie?" It was Livy at the door. Must be afternoon. Mom doesn't leave for work until Livy comes back from school or Dad is back from a shift. They don't leave me alone. They'd been turning away visitors.

"Go away."

"Josh is here."

"Kremens?"

"The one and only." Josh brushed past Livy, strode in, and sat down on the edge of my bed. In the light from the hall, I saw Livy grinning in the doorway.

"Beat it." She made a face, but she still closed the door softly. I fumbled in the darkness to pull the little chain on the nightstand lamp.

"How you doing?" Josh asked.

"What's up?"

"For starters, we've been outed." He barked out a false laugh.

"Yeah, I heard we were caught making out behind Walmart. You come to break up?" I laughed, which hurt.

"Not so funny."

"I thought it was. Aren't you president of the Rainbow Alliance?"

"Vice president."

"Okay. So?"

"They're out to get us."

"You think?"

"I'm serious." He looked serious. "Don't you get it? It's all part of smearing Group and Ms. L. Make everybody forget about guns. Forget about anything that doesn't fit their whites-are-all-right-apple-pie crap. It's how this town works. How America works."

I was really tired of his crap. "Speaking as a white man?"

He ignored that. "We need to make a statement. You know the poet e.e. cummings's line, 'there is some shit I will not take'?"

"Actually, it's 'there is some shit I will not eat.'"

He looked amazed. "How'd you know that?"

"My sister's favorite poem, 'i sing of Olaf glad and big.' She made me memorize it."

"I keep underestimating you," he said.

"What's the statement?"

"Ban automatic weapons."

"This is getting old, Josh. Isn't that how all this got started? Make WAAR in the auditorium in front of the cops? That's not going to fly, not in this town."

"That's if it's only me and the snowflakes talking. But Rhino Rhinehart, football captain, gun owner, that gets attention."

"You just don't know when to quit, do you?"

"When do you quit, Rhino? When somebody gets killed?"

"Is that you, Josh?" Dad was standing in the doorway.

He jumped. "Mr. Rhinehart."

How long had he been standing there?

Dad came in and shook his hand. "Your dad knows you're here?"

"Just leaving, came to see how Rhino's doing."

"Stay for dinner?"

"Thanks, I better get home." He threw me a glance over his shoulder as he hurried out.

"What was that all about?" Dad asked. "If it's about Group, let it go. Gene and I agree we need to distance from that."

"Gene?"

"Kremens, Josh's dad."

I couldn't resist. "You guys buds now?"

He grinned. "Butch Cassidy and the Sundance Kid."

It took me a minute to get the reference to the old western movie. I couldn't decide if I was glad they were doing something for us or annoyed they were having fun doing it.

I came down for dinner. I was feeling better. Livy couldn't stop describing Josh barging into my room. Turns out that Andy, Maddie, and Jamaal had all come over, separately, and when they heard I was lying in a darkened room, they tiptoed out. But not Josh. He doesn't know when to quit.

We met in a conference room in the Presbyterian Church, big wooden armchairs around a huge wooden table. Even the big butts like me had lots of room. Josh claimed the chair at the head of the table and started talking.

"Thanks for coming out. We've got decisions to make today about Group and about our future." His voice was strong, and he made eye contact with each of us. "We've got a chance to make a difference, to start a movement, to wake up a town. Are we all together on this?"

"Count me in," Joy said.

"Could we just slow down a little?" Tyla said. "What exactly are we supposed to be all together on?"

"We've talked about this," Josh said. I didn't like his overpatient tone of voice, like he was talking to a kid. "We've agreed to a Homecoming demonstration as a start to—"

"Whoa," I said. "When did we agree to that?"

"We've discussed it," Josh said. "Now we're discussing preparation. Making sure we organize the school, get media attention . . ."

"Time-out." Tyla made the sign Ms. L used. "You can't hijack Group for your own purposes."

Josh rolled his eyes at her. "You think banning murder weapons is my own purposes?"

"Yeah," Marco said. "It's not why we're here."

Dead silence. You could hear a pin drop. I understood those cliches. When Marco speaks, everybody listens.

Josh glared at him. "What's your point?"

"It's Group," Marco said. "We're trying to help each other figure out who we are and what's going on."

"We still are," Joy said, "but Ms. L's not here so it's up to us."

"Let's get real here," Tyla said. "The original idea of Group was an alternative to juvie or worse so people could share their issues in a safe environment. And it was starting to happen."

"Maybe," Josh said, "but the school used it to stash a bunch of misfits in a corner so they'd be out of sight and it could say it was doing something. And look what happened."

"What happened," Marco said, "is you walked in . . ."

"This is not helpful," Josh said. He sounded like he was losing his cool. "We need to be a team."

I thought, Yeah, right. Go, Vikings. "A team has a purpose," I said. "All on the same page. What's that, Josh?"

"Whatever we want," Josh said.

"Maybe we should vote," Marco said.

Josh must have figured he'd lose any kind of vote. "Let's talk some more after . . ."

There was a tap on the door, then Pastor Bill poked his head in.

He was a smiley guy everybody liked. "You all okay here?" I wondered what he had heard through the door.

"We're planning," Josh said. Big phony smile.

"Sounds promising," Pastor Bill said. "No surprises now. This is a church."

"The civil rights movement came out of churches," Josh said.

Pastor Bill nodded at Josh. "That's true. But for now, we hope you'll continue in the spirit of Group, of Ms. L's vision of mutual support . . ."

"That may no longer be enough," Josh said.

"I understand," Pastor Bill said. "I'm gratified to see your generation stepping up in places my generation has failed. But your political activities need to be separate from those connected to Group or this church."

"How can human rights be separated from Group or church?" Joy asked.

"We're just trying to keep you out of trouble," Pastor Bill said. "Those police charges are still pending."

Pastor Bill turned to me. "How are you feeling?"

"I'm good. Doctor cleared me for light practice."

"Excellent. But don't rush it." He waved on his way out. "So glad you're all here."

Josh waited until Pastor Bill was gone. "Just what's on your mind, Tyla?"

He said it sharply enough that Tyla blinked. "I think we need to get back to what Group is about."

"We're beyond that now," Josh said. "We have existential issues. Like stopping the killing. Banning assault rifles."

"That's an issue that affects us all," Joy said. She looked around, daring anybody to challenge Josh and her.

The five of us weren't on the same page. Josh and Joy had something cooking, Tyla and Marco were pushing back. Rhino was the wild card. Meanwhile I'd really like to know what was on Tyla's mind. And what was going on with Marco. What had gotten to him? Woken him up? Hey, is that what the word really means?

Josh punted. He called for an adjournment. Joy seconded it, and the meeting broke up. I left first. Mom was waiting to drive me to practice. She said she didn't want me bouncing around in my truck with its worn-out shocks, but I think she just wanted to hang on to me as long as she could. Mom doesn't come across as super-emotional, but she cares a lot. The concussion shook her up. She'd never been that much into football. After the NFL brain trauma cover-up came out, she found it hard to watch football on TV. She'd walk out of the room after a hard hit.

When the team doctor cleared me for light noncontact workouts, she insisted on a second opinion from the family doctor, who agreed with her that I should stay off the field for a couple more days. But Dad and Coach insisted I show up for walk-throughs and video sessions. The compromise was no lifting, sprints, or calisthenics, just gentle stretches. Everybody kept asking if my headaches were all gone. They were, I lied.

She parked at the edge of the field. Coach walked over. Mom rolled down her window.

"Valerie, good to see you." He peered into the car at me. "How's the head, son?"

"Hard and ready, Coach."

"What I like to hear."

"Ronnie will just observe today."

"We can do that, Valerie." He was placating her. Mom would snap at Dad when he used that tone of voice on her.

"I'm counting on it, Glenn," she said. I was glad she didn't snap at him, then disappointed. What did I want? "Ronnie, call me when you're ready to go home."

"I'll get a ride."

"Better not be on Andy's scooter."

I got out of the car and followed Coach onto the field as Mom pulled away.

He chuckled. "Never get between Mama Bear and her cub." Dickhead.

The guys welcomed me back carefully, no hard bumps or slaps, nothing near my head. Cogan and his Berserkers kept their distance. Domi, Jamaal, Justin, and a couple other guys formed a pocket around me as we walked through plays. Nobody gets close enough to jostle Captain Rhino.

The hardest part was watching videos. My eyes blurred and stung when the picture got very bright. I felt dizzy. I could live with it, but I wasn't sure how much hard information was getting through. I stayed in the audiovisual room when the team went back to the locker room. Andy sat down next to me.

"Sure you're not pushing it?"

"I'm fine." My head was throbbing. "Hey, drive me home?"

"I got the scooter. I'll get Domi or Justin."

While I was waiting outside, Cogan walked slowly past me, grinning. "What do you hear from your head?"

I just grinned back. Someday soon you'll find out.

NINETEEN

WE PASSED A DOZEN HANDMADE MAKE WAAR SIGNS IN downtown Woodhaven as we drove to the interstate on the way to Gramps and Gramma. Josh had been busy. I wondered how long the Berserkers would let the signs stay up.

"This'll burn out," Dad said. "We're learning how to contain it. A real problem on campus. You can't ignore it or overreact. And you have to keep the sides apart."

"How do you do that?" Livy asked. She was in the back with Mom, who was going through real estate listings on her iPad.

"Show up in force. Keep the outside rabble-rousers outside."

"It gives the town a bad image," Mom said. "Affects property values."

"All we need is one of those radical groups to get involved," Dad said. "Black Lives Matter, the gun control snowflakes . . ."

"Gun control snowflakes?" Livy squawked.

"Just making sure you're . . . woke." Dad laughed.

"What's that word even mean?" Mom asked. She hardly ever gets involved in political discussions.

"Where've you been, Val?" Dad said. "It describes know-it-all elites who want to change American history and our basic values."

"Like what?" Livy asked.

"You writing a paper for some liberal teacher, too?" Dad said, trying to laugh off the question.

"It's a good question." I said it sharply enough to surprise myself and set Dad back a beat.

"Okay," he said. "All this white guilt, everything bad that's happened is our fault and we need to make it up to the minorities."

"Like slavery?" Livy asked. She had an edge to her voice. I liked it. Way past where I was at her age. Maybe even now.

"That was a long time ago. You ever patrol in a minority neighborhood, the crime and drugs and . . ."

"Maybe they never got a chance to get on their feet after slavery, and then segregation kept people down," I said. That was in the books I've been reading. I felt Livy's little fist chop my shoulder. Go, bro.

"A chance? You notice how many Black NFL quarterbacks there are now?" Dad asked.

"How many Black senators?" Livy asked. If I hadn't been strapped in, I would have given her a high five.

"Team owners," I added.

"See what I mean?" Dad said. "Brainwashing in the schools."

"Music. Please!" Mom said.

Dad poked the radio button. Country, of course.

Livy and I put on our headphones. I was listening to Drake's new album, *Views*, the last gift from Maddie before we broke up. It wasn't his best. Or maybe my tastes are changing.

I slept through most of the ride. As a kid, I looked forward to visiting Gramps and Gramma, loved the animals, shooting guns and bows, but once I got into high school ball, I didn't always make the trips. It's at least a two-hour ride each way.

I woke up to Gramps's grinning face. He was tapping at my window. Big hugs. Gramps and Gramma seemed smaller, bonier than last time. I was afraid I'd crack a rib.

Gramps was pushing eighty, but he insisted on our pre-meal ritual of passing a football, semi-deflated so he got a better grip. He'd been a quarterback and a pitcher in high school and would have gone to college on scholarship if his dad hadn't died. He had to stay home and work the farm. He pushed my dad hard to play and was disappointed when he tore up his knee. Then Dad pushed me.

"Your spiral's not so tight," he said to me.

"Blow up the ball, Gramps. I'm not Tom Brady."

He laughed himself into a coughing fit. Must still be smoking behind the barn. He hated Tom Brady and the Patriots. Deflategate, when Tom was accused of letting the air out of footballs for a better grip, was still a hot topic with him. Those arguments were a lot more fun than the ones he had with Alison over politics.

At dinner, Gramps brought up the shooting. He subscribed to some conspiracy website that claimed Keith had targeted the debate team because they were defending a conservative position on the internet. Wish I could have told him the truth.

"Bit of a stretch, Pop," Dad said. After three beers, he was ready to take on his old man, who started to redden up. Gramps had had a few himself.

"Don't you see what's going on?" Gramps said. "They start

peddling socialism early, so it seems normal."

"Start peddling paranoia, Pops, so shooting up schools seems normal." Dad's always a surprise. You can never be sure what side he's going to take, or if he'll come up with his own off the wall just to take over the conversation. I'd heard he was a top police interrogator because he knew how to keep subjects off balance.

I decided to play captain, defuse the situation. "Speaking of shooting. For dishes?"

They both looked relieved. Mom gave me a thumbs-up.

I didn't exactly tank the shoot-off, but I didn't spend as much time sighting as I should have, especially to clear the blur out of my eyes. I'd been firing Gramps's old .22's since I was eight and they weren't being kept in such good condition anymore. Dad talked him out of bringing out the AR-15 and the Czech sniper rifle. Gramps was cackling through his final shots when Dad and I had no chance to catch up. I think Dad was tanking the shoot-off, but he beat me.

I didn't mind doing the dishes while Gramps and Dad napped before ice cream and pie on the porch. Mom and Gramma, who is kind of fading mentally, did some sewing on the old Singer machine.

Livy came in and offered to help. "So how come Keith didn't know they changed the room?"

"Where you hear that?" I tried to sound casual. The kid picks up stuff.

"It's around."

"Last-minute change." I tossed her a towel.

"In my school, someone would have waited for anyone not there yet or at least left a note. Why didn't the teacher . . ."

"She did. She put a note up." I have to defend you, Ms. L. "Maybe he didn't see it. Or it fell off."

"Or somebody ripped it down."

I held my breath. "Why?"

"Like, who wanted Keith around? I heard he was a real creep."

"I heard that, too."

"Hey." She whipped the towel back at me. "You were in Group with him, you knew him. What was he like?"

"Nasty mouth, never shut up." I thought of his Rhino sketch. "He was a good artist."

"I heard he got bullied a lot. Football players, of course."

"Who are you talking to?" I asked. "Josh?"

"He was outside school, giving out leaflets for a demonstration."

"Recruiting little kids?"

"Eighth graders are not little kids."

Mom walked in. "Need a hand? We're leaving soon."

"I gotta say goodbye to the chickens," Livy said.

I remembered how Alison used to make remarks when I played with the piglets and gave them names. She'd say, *Hope you remember who's who when you're eating them next year.*

"Don't name the chickens," I said to Livy.

"Why?"

"Harder to eat them."

"That's why I'm a vegetarian," she said very seriously. That kid leaves me in the dust.

Mom waited until Livy was out of the kitchen before she said, "You were blinking a lot when you were shooting. Your eyes bothering you?"

"They're fine."

"Thank God you're a lousy liar. We need to see the doctor again."

"It just wasn't as much fun. Shooting. Since, you know."

She gave me a hug. "It's been a hard time for you, Ronnie. Every-body's pulling on you."

"I'm okay," I said.

"I know you can handle it. I'm just sorry you have to." She hugged tighter. It felt good but somehow it made me think things were even worse than I thought.

Standing at the car waiting to go, watching Gramps hug Livy good-bye the way he used to hug Alison, I surprised myself by saying, "Hey, Gramps, Alison sends her regards."

"Yeah? How is she?"

"She's good. She's managing a shelter for old dogs."

He looked sad for a moment, like he was remembering a time when Alison was small. Then his face got hard again. "Well, that's better than picking up poop for that other bitch." He laughed into another coughing fit.

When nobody reacted, he said, "I'm talking about Crooked Hil-lary. Last time I saw Alison she was wearing one of those 'A woman's place is in the House and Senate' buttons."

"Saddle up," Dad said. "Want to beat the traffic."

Gramps said, "Know who I like? Donald Trump."

"Never win," Livy said. "He's a stupid clown."

"When he said he could stand in the middle of Fifth Avenue in New York City and shoot somebody without losing any votes, I knew he was my man." Gramps grinned and threw a fist.

Dad started shoving us toward the car.

Bad Sunday traffic on the ride home took forever, especially since I couldn't sleep.

Mom was right. Everybody's pulling on me. But I'm not so sure

I can handle it all. Josh wants me to join his gang, and Cogan wants me to go away. Maddie wants to get back together. What does Tyla want? What do I want?

I have to talk to Andy about this project. I need to do something for Mr. Biedermann to stay eligible. Isn't staying on the team still what this is all about?

How did Tyla get into this?

TWENTY

JOSH WAS ALREADY TALKING WHEN I SHOWED UP AT Group. He shut up when I walked in. Something I'm not supposed to hear?

"Am I interrupting something?"

"As a matter of fact," Josh said, "we're planning an event."

"You're still pushing your little Homecoming march," I said.

"It'll get attention," Joy said. "Wake people up."

"It's going to pull people apart," I said. "You want a civil war?"

"The last one ended slavery," Joy said.

"I don't think this is what Ms. Lamusciano had in mind for Group," I said.

"She's gone," Josh said. "It's our Group now."

"It's your Group," I said, and walked out. I was in the church parking lot before Tyla caught up to me.

"We need you."

"For what?"

She had my arm in a strong grip. I remembered her fingers clawing into my thigh, holding me back from going after Josh when he called me a fascist. Seemed like a long time ago.

"Josh has his agenda, Ronnie. But he isn't all wrong. If the two of you work together . . ."

"Why should I—"

"Because it's the right thing."

The way she said it, her intense ocean-gray eyes wide, made me hot and cold. She had changed her look, I noticed—the crazy hair pulled back, a touch of makeup, clothes that were tighter around a slim but curvy body. Some of the piercings were gone.

"How are you so sure?"

She pulled me around to a little flower garden alongside the church, and onto a wooden bench.

"I'm not really sure of anything," she said. "But I think you're an okay guy. I think you mean well, and if we don't do something, who will?"

"You think it's going to make a difference?"

She shrugged. "Won't know unless we try."

"I don't trust Josh a hundred percent," I said.

"Hey, I don't trust anybody fifty percent."

"Me too?" That just popped out. I held my breath, expecting a smart-ass reaction, but she smiled.

"That's another conversation." She stood up. "Let's go hear Josh out."

"Wait." I stood up. "What about your last chance? What about not blowing it?"

"I can't just think about myself anymore."

I followed her inside.

Josh nodded when we walked in. "Just saying, there'll be groups from Nearmont and Ridgefield Park. Maybe a few other high schools, including a couple from the city. Enough to get TV, for sure."

"What about counterdemonstrators?" I asked.

He shrugged. "That's out of our hands."

"You're counting on them, aren't you?" I said. "Get you more publicity. Need some of those Loud Boys."

"Be great if there was no opposition, right?" Josh said. "Everybody on the same page, no automatic weapons, who needs them unless you plan on robbing people or overthrowing the government? But what do all these guns tell you?"

"People like them," I said. "Shooting is fun, it's a right."

"A right to come into school blasting away? Think how close we came."

"What's your plan?" Marco asked. It was still a shock to hear him speak after all his silence. With the hood of his dark blue sweatshirt pulled back, you could actually see his big round brown face.

"Simple," Josh said. "Just people marching around the ball field at halftime carrying signs. We'll have a few information tables set up to sign petitions and join gun control groups."

"Don't you need permission?" Tyla asked.

"Never get it. We can probably make a couple of circuits before the cops push us off. But we'll be seen by then, points made."

"What about Mr. Biedermann and Ms. Lamusciano, shouldn't they get a heads-up?" Tyla asked.

"And put them in a tough spot?" Josh said. "They should have deniability. If they don't know what's going to happen, they're not accountable. It's on us."

Maybe my mind was still fogged, but I didn't quite get it. "This is Mr. Biedermann's church and in people's minds still Ms. L's Group," I said. "They'll get blamed even if they haven't been informed beforehand."

"Ronnie's right," Tyla said. "This is still Group. We're here to create a safe place to support each other."

"What's safer than a gun-free environment?" Josh asked.

"A Josh-free environment?" Marco said.

"Marco's hardly opened his mouth since day one," Josh said. "Now all of a sudden he's . . ."

"You haven't been here since day one," Marco said. "You just marched in and tried to hijack the program. I want to hear what Ron has to say."

Everybody turned to me. I felt like I was suddenly Group Captain. "Okay, Rhino," Josh said. "What do you have to say?"

It sounded like a challenge.

"I don't think it's a good time to go against the school or the town when they're down," I said. "People are hurting. There'll be plenty of time to demonstrate, to campaign against guns."

"After the next shooting?" Josh said.

"You're right, people have to get out there and make a statement, but waiting a couple more weeks isn't going to make that much of a difference. And it might even let things cool down so people are willing to listen."

The way even Joy was looking back and forth between Josh and me, I could tell I had scored some points. I kept going. "I think information tables near the entrance to the field is a good idea. But nothing that's going to provoke a reaction."

"You never know what provokes a reaction," Josh said.

"You can be sure if you're marching for gun control without permission at a football game," Tyla said.

"And it's Homecoming," I said. "After a shooting. We really need to give the school a chance to heal, to come together."

That hit home. Even Joy nodded. Marco gave me a thumbs-up.

The meeting broke up soon after that. There'd be another one in a couple of days. On the way out, I thought Tyla was trying to catch my eye, so I pretended to fix my laces so she could catch up, but it was Josh who grabbed me.

Tyla turned the corner. Too late.

"I thought we were together on this," Josh said.

"You must be the one with the concussion."

"This is an opportunity we can't pass up. And what about Keith?"

"He's in jail, right?"

"Not for much longer. He's going to get moved to a psychiatric hospital. I think we should reach out to him."

"What?"

"In the spirit of Group. Think of it, all of us pushed into the same box because we weren't playing their game, even you, perfect white boy football hero, has to be slapped down along with me. There is shit we will not eat."

"C'mon. Keith wanted to kill us."

"We don't know what was on his mind. We should talk to him."

"I don't think so." My head was hurting. I looked for my truck before I remembered Mom had insisted I take her car.

I found it sitting on its rims with all four tires slashed.

TWENTY-ONE

THE FIRST COP WHO RESPONDED SAID HE'D PLAYED
for Woodhaven a few years back and the same thing happened to
him. Over a girl. He gave me a high five. Dumb jock cop.

Dad arrived with the chief and more cops, and they took it seriously. Pastor Bill was an important guy in Woodhaven. Slashed tires
in his parking lot was not a good look for church business.

The chief wanted to know if anybody had a beef with me.

"Talk to John Cogan," Dad said.

"He's on the team," said the chief. "What about Josh Kremens?
His jaw probably still hurts."

"He was inside the church with me," I said.

"Doing what?" The chief's eyes narrowed, as if he was interview-
ing a perp on a TV cop show.

"Group," I said. "In lieu of detention."

"Oh, yeah." He seemed disappointed.

Dad drove me home. He was steaming. "This gun control crap is not going to fly in this town, Ronnie. Maybe it'll help get Josh into some Ivy League college, but no SEC coach is looking for a trouble-maker."

"What's gun control got to do with this?" I asked.

"You think I don't know what you're planning with Josh?" he asked.

"Is that what you and Butch Cassidy talk about?"

He laughed all the way home, dropped me off, and left for his mall job.

Mom was ticked off. She counts on her car for work and was not happy about having to show up at an open house in my truck. Also, slashed tires were not good for business. House hunters would ask, *What kind of town is Woodhaven?*

Good question. Beats me. I've never lived anywhere else, but Woodhaven doesn't make the cut for top towns. I don't think it even tries. The nearest big city is New York, a couple of hours away, but I've only been there a few times, class trips to museums and the Broadway theater, some pro games. Pretty exciting. Like most people in town, Mom and Dad don't go to the city much, they think it's dirty and dangerous, but I'd love to live there, especially if I was play-ing for the Jets or the Giants.

There are no big-time college football programs near New York. I'd like to play near a big city, Miami or LA would be cool. It's pos-sible. I've had recruiting feelers from Miami, UCLA, and USC, among a bunch of others, but no solid offers yet, no calls from a head coach, just lots of suggestions that I step up my lifting routine. Get bigger. Like they're thinking lineman while I'm thinking linebacker. The letters I want, telling me to get faster, more explosive, mostly come from my second choice Division I schools and from Division

II and some Division III. I've got Honor Roll grades, so I even got a letter from Columbia, which is right in New York City, but how many pros come out of there?

How I do this year is important. Coming from a mid-level high school program, I'll need a decent ranking on next year's ESPN 300 to get noticed by the power colleges. Some monster plays that go viral would do it. One of my dreamy Rhino's Runs. Also, it would help to win some games, and get some publicity.

I can understand Dad's thinking on this, just hang tough and keep moving, make yourself into the best baller you can be. Stay alert, pay attention to the coaches, watch the video, lift, run, play smart. And I do all that. But sometimes I wonder if I do enough and if I'm doing it with passion. That's an Alison word. She used to talk about finding things to be passionate about, to really care about, to want to do, whether it pays off or not. To love the process even more than the prize.

And that's my problem, Ms. L. I love to play football, to hit and run, to figure stuff out, to make things happen, to beat other guys. And I love that football is going to be my ticket out.

But football isn't the only thing I want to do. I'd love to be in another school play. I'd like to read more. I'd like to do a documentary with Andy, and I have to admit I'm even getting a kick out of writing this ridiculous thing. I wonder where it's going to go. How much I'll spill out.

So, what's it all mean, Ms. L? You're the psychologist. And you have this idea of Group as a team. Really? A football team is a bunch of guys who share a cause—winning—and when they win, they mostly like each other. Same for the fans, coaches, school, town. The team is there to represent them, win for them. If we don't, we're losers and they hate us because they don't want to think they're losers, too.

Group is different. It's supposed to be about helping each other through tough times. It's not about getting hijacked into some cause. Certainly not about killing each other.

Maybe reaching out to Keith isn't so crazy. Why does he think the way he does? Just a screw loose, or something in society that affects him more than it affects other people? Can we help him?

Heavy thinking.

Practice felt different. First off, I still wasn't cleared for full contact, and Coach made me wear a red singlet just so everyone else understood that. And once the guys treat you a little differently, you aren't part of the team anymore. They even talk to you differently, like more *gently,* if that makes any sense, like you're breakable. Also, that you're not really one of them. They don't want to bump into you, even with hard words, so it's like you're in a bubble everyone's avoiding. And what was truly weird was that I wasn't really bothered by it.

I mean usually, for example, I feel so electric waiting for football practice that if I stuck a plug up my rectum I could charge all my devices. I feel jittery little wires running up my arms and legs and the main cable from my brain pulses down through my chest and stomach. Working out doesn't help much, not even running or lifting. What keeps me going is knowing how much better I'll feel when contact starts. I need to hit. Get hit.

But I'm not feeling it. Maybe it's an aftereffect of the ding. Maybe it's something else. It comes with a little sadness, too, like I'm missing something. Falling out of love with football?

Sucking noises in the defensive huddle. Cogan's grinning at me, lips puckered. Perlick and Belfer, too. It took me a few beats to tune it in. They were throwing me kisses. Qualifies as a gay slur, I guess. Is that the best they can do? Probably not. The slashed tires. Want to make them pay for that. But I can wait until I have extra energy. And some proof. Andy is going to check the cameras around the church parking lot.

After practice, Coach called me into his office. Colligan and Dixon were there.

"You okay?" Coach asked. "Seemed a little drifty out there."

"I'm good, Coach. Saving it for contact tomorrow."

"Glad to hear that." He looked at Dixon, who said, "So what's with you and Josh Kremens?"

I felt something like bile or vomit come up in my throat. I think I came close to saying something like, Yeah, we're gay, like you and Dixon. Loud and proud.

Maybe I came close or maybe I'm just giving myself bigger balls than I deserve. All I said was "We're in Group together."

Coach looked at Colligan, who cleared his throat and growled, "We know that. What else is going on?"

I just shook my head, which didn't hurt. That was good.

"Josh is president of the Rainbow Alliance," said Colligan.

"Vice president," I said.

They looked at each other. Colligan said, "Nothing wrong with that, but what does that tell you?"

"That he's a politician," I said. "He belongs to the Red Cross Club, the Key Club, the Film Club, the Science Fiction Society, the . . ."

"We get it," Coach said. "Are you defending him?"

"I'm explaining him," I said, and I let my voice get frosty. It felt like I was standing up to the coaches, an all-time first. "I didn't choose to be in Group with him. I didn't stick me there."

That put a little smile on Coach's face. I think he likes light pushbacks. Just enough to know you're reacting to him, not enough to challenge his authority. "Go get your rest, Rhino. Tomorrow, you get to hit, you'll feel better." He waved me out. I guess he figures he still has me by the short hairs, as Dad would say. And as long as football is all I care about, he does. That might be changing.

The locker room was clear except for Andy. "You okay?"

"You always say that."

"What should I say?"

"Sorry. Didn't mean to let it out on you."

"No problem. Lots coming down on you. What did the coaches say?"

"Brought up Josh."

"They're at the end of their rope. Season's going down the drain and they lost control of Cogan."

"They gave him control," I said. "The team, the school."

"What are we going to do?"

"I'm going to suck it up and wait it out. He'll be gone. Next year's our time."

"If we get there, Ronnie." Andy's face was getting red. "Cogan's desperate, he's going off the deep end, and you're cruising along, thinking you're gonna get your ticket punched and be all right. Don't be so sure. And what about everybody else, the kids he's beaten up, the kids he's gonna beat up. Who's gonna stop him, stop the school from just rolling over for him?" He gasped for breath. "Tell me we don't have to do something, Captain."

"Like what?"

"A documentary. Our documentary. For Mr. Biedermann, but

really for the whole school. Tell it like it is."

"And then what?"

"Who knows?" Andy said. "But at least we did something. We didn't just try to ride it out. You know, it's not just about you, Ronnie. You think Coach is going to like the documentary? Dr. Mullins? You think they're going to recommend me to film school?"

After a while, I said, "I never should have let you copy my math answers."

He grinned. We fist bumped.

TWENTY-TWO

I WAS STILL SITTING THERE WHEN YOU CALLED.

"Ronnie? How are you feeling? I heard about the concussion."

"I'm fine, Ms. L. Cleared to play."

"That's good. Look, I have some . . . disturbing news. Keith left the facility where he had been assigned."

"Left?"

"Well, escaped."

"You think he's coming after us?"

"I don't think there's anything to worry about, but just be alert. I'll get back as soon as I know more. I need to call the others." She hung up.

Did Keith have a gun? Was he coming after the Group? Or just me? Why wasn't I feeling more scared?

Josh called. "You heard?"

"Yeah."

"Group in an hour. Keith's going to be there."

"What?"

"He just called me. He wants to apologize. Says it was a terrible mistake. He'll explain everything."

"You trust him?"

"I do."

"He wants to turn himself in?"

"I don't know. It makes sense to get him back into the Group, talk him down, get him back into safe custody."

"Does he have a gun?"

"I don't think so."

"Think so?"

"You can ask him."

"Great. What about the cops? Did you call them?"

"I promised him I wouldn't. Give him a chance to talk."

"To kill people this time."

"To explain himself. He's sorry. We have to do this."

"Why?"

"You coming or not?"

I took a deep breath. Did I have a choice? Captain. "The church?"

"There's a back door by the garbage bins. Park down by the nature preserve and come through Haven Wood." He hung up.

Tyla opened the back door from the inside before I touched the outside knob. She led me into a large storeroom in the church basement. I wanted to talk to her, but there was no time. The Group was waiting, sitting on the folding wooden chairs the church brings out for outdoor events. Tense and quiet.

Keith looked different. He was clean shaven. His wild mop of hair had been sheared down into a preppy cut except where there was a long reddish-brown scab from his gunshot wound. He was wearing jeans, a white sweatshirt, running shoes.

He stood up when I came in. "I'm very sorry, Ron."

I felt confused. This wasn't Keith. For a moment I thought, Sorry for what? "Why did you want to kill me?"

"I never wanted to kill anybody." His voice was soft. He seemed very calm. "I wanted to scare you."

"Why?"

"To leave me alone." He was looking down, wheezing.

"I never touched you. I don't think I ever talked to you before Group."

"Football captain. You were sent to get me."

"Who sent me?" I knew.

"Cogan. He told me that." He was crying.

"He lied."

"You didn't stop them," Keith said.

I felt sick. "I'm sorry."

"C'mon, that was before Ronnie's time," Tyla said. "They bullied you for years."

"Then you showed up at Group," Keith said to me. "I was feeling safe in Group. It was like you were coming after me."

"This is not fair," Tyla said. "Ronnie just got to be captain. Cogan and his thugs are a year ahead of us."

I didn't know what to say. It was true that I had never tried to stop Cogan.

"What do you want, Keith?" Marco asked.

"I don't think I ever heard you talk before," Keith said.

"You talked a lot."

"I'm taking some meds now."

"Why are you here?" I asked.

"Help me get away."

The room got very quiet. "Do you have a gun?" I asked.

Keith shook his head. "Didn't mean to shoot anybody, just scare you."

"You did that," Tyla said. People laughed. It broke the tension in the room.

"What do you mean, get away?" I asked. "Where would you go?"

"Out of town. A safe place."

"They'll come after you," Josh said. "You'll be a fugitive."

"Better than a prisoner."

"As a patient," Joy said, "you'll get help."

"Cogan, the cops, they'll kill me if I stay here." Keith was shaking. "No place here for people like me."

"People like us," Joy said. "We're here together to support each other. We'll be here for you."

"All of us," I said. Tyla smiled at me. I felt a warm flush through my body. I liked the idea of helping Keith.

"You can't run away," I said. "But you can work things out."

"They won't let me."

"We'll be here for you," I said. "We'll be your pocket."

"What's that?" Keith asked.

"It's football," Marco said. "When the team protects the . . ."

There were two taps on the storeroom door, a pause, then three taps. It sounded like a signal.

Josh opened the door for Ms. L.

Keith ran into her arms and started to sob.

The cops burst in behind her.

They were screaming, "Face the walls, hands up!"

The cops shoved us against the walls. I felt a baton rammed into my back. When I turned, I was hit in the face.

I saw one of the cops ram his baton into Keith's chest. He started gasping. Keith reached into his pocket, pulled out his black inhaler.

"Gun!" a cop screamed.

"Inhaler." I couldn't get the word out fast enough. I lunged toward Keith but never got there. A baton slammed into the back of my head. As I went down, I heard shots.

I don't remember much about the rest of that night. My mind kept blinking on and off. Keith's body went into an ambulance and the chief ordered me into a patrol car, but Dad said he would drive me to the station, and there was some yelling and pushing, but I ended up in Dad's car. He didn't want to let me out of his sight. He wouldn't say it, but I could tell he didn't trust the cops. He drove with one hand on the wheel, one gripping my arm.

It was a dumpster fire at the police station. Ms. L and the Group were there, Dr. Mullins, parents, Mr. Kremens, Mr. Biedermann, all kinds of cops, everybody yelling.

I was hustled into an interview room with the detective sergeant. Dad bulled his way in. When the detective tried to block him, Dad said that I was a minor and could not be interviewed without a parent or legal representative present.

There was more yelling, and my headache came back, blotting out most everything. It's the next day as I dictate this, and I'm remembering fragments like falling forward, banging my forehead on the table, and Dad saying, "We're done here," just like on TV. Then the screen faded to black.

TWENTY-THREE

I WAS COOKING IN A HOT BATH, TRYING TO RELAX MY hammies, when Dad knocked on the door and walked in. "Chief wants to talk to you."

"Again? What about?"

"What Keith said to the Group about getting killed by the cops."

"We talked about that already."

He sat on the toilet seat. "Gene is putting pressure on the town. Says it wasn't a justified shooting."

"It wasn't."

"He was reaching for something," Dad said.

"An inhaler."

"How would they know?"

"They wanted to shoot him."

"That's not true." He didn't sound convinced himself.

"You think it was justified?"

"You have to make decisions at warp-speed . . ." Dad sighed. "Hey, just talk to the chief, okay? Don't make it personal." He stood up.

"How did they show up so quick?" I asked.

"They got a tip."

"From who?"

"I like the shrink for that," Dad said. "Legally, she was supposed to."

"Turning in a patient before she had a real chance to talk to him?"

He shrugged. "The cops came in with her. To protect her."

"More like they rushed the door and pushed in behind her."

"Maybe they thought it was a hostage situation."

"What does she say?"

Dad shook his head. "She's not talking. Look, Ronnie, just don't say too much, play dumb. If they want to bring you guys down, they can bust you for harboring a fugitive, which is a felony."

"Why would they want to bring us down?"

"They want to keep the school and the town clean. They'll try to keep the focus on the Group and Ms. Lamusciano." There was noise downstairs. Mom and Livy were back. "Use the concussion. Tell the chief your mind's not clear."

That's for sure.

Josh called late, woke me up. He wanted me to run security for Keith's memorial at Haven Park. He said there might be trouble. People in the community were against the memorial, and the chief refused to issue a permit because of "public safety concerns." Josh read me a story online in the *Woodhaven Gazette* that quoted Cogan as saying the Berserkers would be at the park to block anyone from "honoring that animal."

I said I'd be there. I texted Andy, Jamaal, Domi, Justin, and a few other guys.

I thought of calling Tyla. Not ready for that. Ready for what?

TWENTY-FOUR

I WAS WAY EARLY TO HAVEN PARK, BUT ANDY WAS already there checking camera angles. He'd bought a half-dozen phones and set them up in bushes and trees, then covered them with camouflage cloths. He could operate them remotely.

"You look like dog food, partner," he said.

"Hello to you, too."

"I'm serious, Ron. You okay?"

"Fine."

"How can you be fine? You were there. He was killed right in front of you."

"It feels like a movie clip. It didn't have to happen."

"Cogan says someone in the Group grabbed Keith's gun and hid it."

"There was no gun. He was reaching for an asthma inhaler."

"Cogan's trying to get some upstate militia groups," Andy said.

"How do you know that?"

"My sources." I knew he had hacker friends. He looked around and lowered his voice. "Got some video I want you to see. For Andiron."

"Andiron?"

"Our documentary. *WoodhavenReal!*"

"Are you for real?"

"Look." He came up close, almost nose to nose. Not like him. "Something bad happened. We got to tell the story. Can't let them bury it with Keith." I'd never heard cool Andy so passionate about anything.

"Aren't you doing a doc for the school?"

He made a face. "That's for Dr. Mullins. *WoodhavenStrong!* Makes me feel like Leni Riefenstahl."

"Who?"

"She did propaganda films for Hitler."

"You been talking to Josh?"

He shook his head. "Don't need to. You with me?"

He held out his fist to bump. I covered his fist with my hand. "What are we doing?"

"We're going to connect the dots. Football, Cogan, the school, Keith, and stick it in their faces."

I felt lost. "Is this for Mr. Biedermann?"

"It's for everybody." The way he said it started an ice ball. I bumped his fist.

Jamaal, Domi, and Justin showed up with five other guys from the team. Big hugs. I felt proud to have such teammates. Friends.

Josh came out of the woods with a bunch of Woodhaven kids. He raised a fist. I raised one back. They came over.

Domi whispered, "We rolling with them?"

"We're on the same side," I said.

Domi pulled a face.

"Chill," Jamaal snapped. "Today we're on the same side. See how it goes. Decide again tomorrow."

"That's good enough," I said. "I think we should spread out around the front and sides of the band shell. Don't let anybody rush the stage."

Jamaal laughed. "Like last time. Who you get to punch today, Cap?"

I faked a short right. Justin pretended he'd been hit. Everybody laughed. Just like the locker room. That's good.

Tyla marched up. She put a hand on my arm. "I was so sure you were going to get shot, too. The way the cops came in, looking wild, maybe scared."

"Cops always say they're scared," Jamaal said. "That's how they get off killing people."

"Let's get this organized," Josh said, all business. "I'll go first, intro the speakers. You guys want to say anything? Rhino?"

I thought of Keith's last words. "He wanted us to help him get away. He said there was no place here for people like him."

"It was sad and powerful," Tyla said. "Ron should say it."

"It fits into my eulogy," Josh said.

"Doesn't everything," Tyla said, rolling her eyes.

Ms. L and Mr. Biedermann showed up holding candles. They waved and took seats near the front of the band shell. We waited as people filled the benches. Dozens of flickering lights in the dusk.

I spotted Cogan, Perlick, Belsky, and some other Berserkers, also some tough-looking dudes I didn't recognize. Beards and camos.

Must be the out-of-towners. Be a helluva brawl if it comes to that. Were they packing? They wove their way through the crowd, which was mostly Woodhaven High students, some parents and teachers, a few TV camera operators and reporters. Maybe a hundred people. Not so many. Was it Keith or was the word out there would be trouble?

Josh went up onstage with his portable mic. I took a position near the stairs leading to the stage and signaled my teammates to fan out around the front. I hit record on my phone.

"Welcome.

"None of us really knew Keith Korn. Or cared about him. That was our fault as much as it was his. We didn't say hello in the hallway and neither did he. We didn't sit next to him in the cafeteria, figuring he'd just move away. He was a talented artist, and we didn't talk to him about his drawings. We all stayed in our little bubbles. Like we always do."

I was impressed. He sounded presidential. Tyla nudged me. I hadn't realized she was standing next to me. Those cold eyes looked warmer, softer.

"We're not here to take the blame or to assign it for the tragedy of Keith's life and death. He was bullied in a system that allowed it, even encouraged it as a way to keep students under control. He was shot to death—unarmed—in a system that glorifies guns as routine problem solvers."

The boos rose out of different parts of the crowd. Cogan's thugs had scattered, making it seem as if there were more of them.

"If it hadn't been so easy to get an AR-15—or any gun—Keith would not have walked into our school carrying one, he would . . ."

The boos rose and were joined by the whirring buzz of a dozen

handheld fans blowing out the candles. The camos had come prepared. Must have done this before. The crowd stirred and vibrated
as people jostled and shoved each other. Scuffles broke out. Some
Berserkers and camo boys moved toward the stage.

Jamaal leaped on the stage and signaled the team to join him.
He yelled, "Pocket," to form around Josh. I started to climb up, but
Domi pulled me out of the way. "Gotta watch your head, man."

The brawl started when Perlick and some camo boys formed
a wedge and charged the pocket. Domi and Jamaal turned shoulder to shoulder to meet the point of the wedge and break it. They
went down in a pile and more guys swarmed the stage. A guy in gray
camos who was wearing gloves with metal knuckles was hammering
Justin. Blood spurted. I climbed on the stage, got behind gray camo,
and yoked him. I was dragging him off stage when a second gray
camo drove a knee into my back and twisted my head. I was losing
my grip when I heard a roar behind me, and the guy let me go. He
flew past me headfirst off the stage.

"You okay?" Marco asked. He grabbed the legs of the guy I had
yoked, and we swung him off the stage.

"You need to go out for football again," I said.

I'd never seen him smile before.

It was over soon. Sirens screamed and the camos and the Berserkers hustled off to the parking lot.

Andy was on the ground, his best video camera in pieces beside
him, but he looked happy. "I got great stuff. Emmy territory."

By the time the cops showed up, the bad guys were gone, the candles
were out, and the crowd was standing around in little clumps. Andy
and I went around talking quietly so the cops wouldn't hear, asking

people to send us any video they had shot of Josh, the crowd, the thugs, the fights. Even old footage from school of Cogan and the Berserkers. We promised them anonymity and that we wouldn't give any to the cops. They wouldn't do squat anyway. But we would. I even told a few kids that I had a production company interested in a documentary about what happened. I said I couldn't reveal any more yet. No lie. We didn't know any more than that. No real plan. Yet. Just great footage.

I kept my phone in my sock in case the cops asked for it. I'd say I lost it in the fight.

I wish I'd had it on record when the chief grabbed Josh and said, "You're lucky I'm not charging you with demonstrating without a permit."

Before Josh could say anything, Jamaal lost his usual cool and said, "And Cogan's lucky you're not charging him with assault and inciting a riot."

The chief slowly turned on Jamaal and took his time before he said, "You even live in my town, young man?"

That shut things down. Everybody knows that Jamaal uses the address of the family that his mother works for as his official residence. He lives in another town. As long as he's one of the best running backs in the county, nobody in Woodhaven has a problem with that. It had been Coach's idea in the first place.

I grabbed Jamaal's arm and started dragging him away. The chief shouted after us, "Rhino, you get yourself down to headquarters tomorrow. We need to talk."

"Yes, sir," I said, and kept walking with Jamaal.

I thought some of us would hang for a while, review what happened as if it were a game, but it seemed as though everybody wanted to get away from the scene as quickly as possible. I looked for Tyla but couldn't find her. I was alone, standing in a litter of dead candles. For some reason, I started picking them up. Maybe I needed to do something, maybe I just didn't like the look of another defeat.

By the time I started walking to my truck, there was only one car left in the parking lot. Ms. L's red Mazda. She was sitting at the wheel, sobbing.

"You okay?"

She shook her head. She was pale, shrunken.

"I'll drive you home," I said.

She nodded.

TWENTY-FIVE

MS. L DIDN'T SAY A WORD ON THE TRIP, MAYBE A HALF hour, just pointing directions with a shaky finger. She lived two towns over in a two-story condo building overlooking a pond. Her apartment was upstairs.

She went into the bathroom, and I eyeballed the little apartment, colorful rugs on the wall, concert posters, and lots of family photos. There were half-packed boxes on the floor.

"Sorry. I really came apart." She looked better, although her smile seemed pasted on. "Something to drink? I mean like water or coffee..."

I thought of her silver thermos. "Green tea?"

"Best thing for you." She was chattering nervously. "Sit down, make yourself comfortable in all this mess."

She went into the kitchen. There was so much clatter I wondered if I should go in to check if she was all right. After a while she came back carrying a tray with mugs of tea, a teapot, milk and honey, and a plate of cookies. She patted the couch for me to sit next to her.

"How are you feeling?"

"Fully recovered, cleared for practice."

"That doesn't mean you're fully recovered, only that they need you." She poured tea, set it on a glass table in front of me.

"No, I'm okay, really." I pointed at the boxes. "Where are you going?"

"Home, for a while."

"We heard you were assigned to another district."

"Well, that's the story." The way her lips clamped shut I could tell she didn't want to talk about it.

"Where's home?"

"Buffalo." She looked down into her tea.

I thought I should probably leave. Started thinking who I would call for a ride back to Woodhaven. I felt awkward here.

"It's none of my business now, but . . . you and Josh are planning something," she said.

"He is. At Homecoming."

"And you?"

I forced a smile. "A couple of touchdowns."

"This has really been tough on you, hasn't it, Ronnie?" She was staring at me with wet eyes.

I shrugged. "Not compared to . . ."

"There are no comparisons; each person suffers alone in their own way. Since the punch, your world has been turned upside down."

I was feeling very uncomfortable. I didn't want to open up all my muddy thoughts about what Andy was planning to do and what I should do about it. "It is what it is."

She smiled. "That doesn't really mean anything, Ronnie. What it is, is how you feel about it. What you want to do about it."

I needed to change the subject. "We'll miss you. You made people feel better. Look at Marco."

"Isn't it wonderful. You were starting to come out of your shell, too."

Enough of that. "Aren't you going to sue them for your job?"

"I already signed an NDA, a nondisclosure agreement. To get severance and avoid prosecution."

"For what?"

Deep breath. "They said they would find something."

"Who's they?"

"The school, the police, the town."

"They're making you take the rap."

She shrugged. "There were red flags, I guess. I didn't see them."

"Like what? He never threatened anybody, never mentioned guns."

"I didn't do my job."

I needed to ask her something. "Did you bring the police to the church?"

She nodded, as if she had been waiting for that. "Once I knew where Keith was, I had to, legally. But I didn't know they were right behind me. They said I could go on ahead and bring him out myself."

"They pushed right in behind you. We all saw that. It wasn't your fault."

"It doesn't matter anymore." She had given up.

"Matters to me," I said.

"Why?"

I felt something start to fall away, like stripping off pads. "It's hard to explain. Sounds kind of silly. But I'm a football captain.

That means something. To me, at least." I felt like I was figuring it out as I went along. "It's my job to keep things honest and fair. It was the reason I punched Josh, but that wasn't really the right thing to do. And there were the things I didn't do. I saw Cogan stuff Keith into a locker last year. Saw other things they did. Never said anything. Just kept my eyes on the prize. For myself."

She leaned toward me. "You're a good boy, Ronnie, on your way to being a good man. You've done the best you can. Now you need to take care of yourself. Play football, get to college. Get out of this town."

"I need to do better than that. I need to tell people what happened, what's been happening here."

"About Keith?"

"About everything. The team, school, the town, the cops."

"How are you going to do that?" Her eyes were so focused on me I was losing breath. I almost told her about Andy's documentary. Maybe my documentary, too, I thought.

All I said was, "I have a plan."

"You have to be very careful. These are people who are determined to keep things the way they are if not roll them back."

"I have to do something," I said. "I pulled off the Post-it you left for Keith."

I felt like the pads had all slid off and iron weights had dropped out of my hands.

She gasped and put a hand on my face. "That's a lot to carry."

We sat like that for a while. Her hand was warm. I could feel her breath. "I'm still writing in my journal."

"I hope you'll keep on doing it."

"I like writing. It woke me up."

"How?"

"I was in a tunnel. Everything was black and white. Couldn't handle ambiguity."

"That sounds like Mr. Biedermann."

"I learned a lot from him. And from you and my sister. From Group."

"I'm so glad to hear that."

"I'm sorry you won't read it."

"Who says?" She rubbed my cheek with her knuckles.

I stood up. "I better go. When are you leaving?"

She smiled. "After the game. I wouldn't want to miss that."

I was outside her condo still trying to figure out who to call for a ride when I got lucky. The county public bus appeared, and I waved it down. The driver recognized me. We talked football all the way to Haven Park, where he went out of his way to drop me off by my truck. Keith never came up in the conversation. Everybody's moving on. The driver wished me luck in the game.

Livy was waiting at the door. Dad hadn't let her go to the memorial; he figured there would be trouble. He cracked a beer and waited while I gave them the highlights, then beckoned me down to the precinct house.

He was sitting in his big leather chair by the time I got down there with an energy drink. He signaled me into one of the slightly smaller leather chairs facing him, one reserved for his cop buddies back when he had them. He toasted me with his beer.

"You did good, son. You're what Gene calls a mensch."

"Mensch?"

"It's a Jewish word, means a solid, dependable man. With

integrity. You've been handling yourself well."

Dad was in a mood I hadn't seen in a long time, probably not since he quit the state troopers. He's been either super edgy, like he's on a case and expecting trouble, or super laid-back, especially after a couple of cold ones.

Now he was relaxed but alert. In control, for a change. Or thinking he was.

"You stayed out with your friends?"

I had a feeling he knew better, so I didn't lie. "I drove Ms. Lamusciano home. She was freaked out."

"Stands to reason. The memorial brought back the shooting. The second trauma is the one that usually gets to you. When's she leaving?"

This was an easy lie to avoid a conversation about Homecoming. "I don't know."

He kept smiling as he talked. "This is a tricky time, and we need to get through it without losing our fix on what's important. Life is complex—we can't always make black-and-white choices. There's a lot at stake here, for you, our family, the school, the town, Ms. Lamusciano, and the rest of the kids in Group. You need to reset, get your focus back on the game. You can't be selfish."

"Selfish? What's more selfish than eyes on the prize?"

"That's not selfish, it's for everybody. You're carrying a lot of people on your shoulders. And you can do it. That's why they made you a captain in the first place. You can stay the course. Like Ali."

"Your hero." I might have rolled my eyes a little.

"Got a better one?"

"For you?" I didn't know how I was talking to Sarge like this. "A Muslim, a Black guy, anti-war . . ."

"All that. But he stood up. For what he believed in. He sacrificed, took the hits. But he didn't let the bastards tell him what to do."

I felt in shock. I just stared at him. Was my mouth open? I wanted to call Alison.

He winked. "Now go work out. You're looking softer."

He wheeled his chair around and turned on his big TV.

I was dismissed. I swallowed back the vomit that came up my throat. The taste of ambiguity. Wasn't Sergeant one of the people who wants to roll everything back like nothing happened?

And then those wild cards, Rhino and Ron. What do they want?

TWENTY-SIX

I NEEDED TO TALK TO HER.

Incredibly, she picked up on the second ring. "What's up, pup?"

"I need some advice."

"Who doesn't?"

I told Alison my plan.

"Are you asking permission?"

"The more I think about it, the crazier it seems," I said.

"Worst-case scenario, it falls flat, you and Andy get kicked out of school, buh-bye football."

"Is there a best case?" I asked.

"It's a great success, you still get kicked out of school, forget Division One."

"How about there's real change, Andy and I both get full scholarships?"

"What are you smoking? Look, whatever you do, be careful."

"That's what Ms. L said."

"Always good advice. How's she doing?" she asked.

"Got kicked out of town."

"Those dudes play rough. What does Sergeant say?"

"Focus on the game."

"Of course."

"But he also said to hang in there. Like Ali."

"That's not so ambiguous. Ali controlled his narrative. Ali didn't get railroaded into doing what he was told. So you have to make a decision."

"Thanks a lot for the help."

"What do you want?" she asked.

"Tell me what you think I should do."

There was a pause. I wondered if she had hung up. "Okay, Ronnie, answer a question. Why are you even thinking about this in the first place?"

"Because it's the right thing to do."

"There you go." She hung up.

Dr. Mullins called a special assembly to show Andy's ten-minute film, *WoodhavenStrong!* It looked professional, just what you would have expected, lots of flags and football, shots of kids at school hanging out happy before the first shooting, then crying and hugging, the assemblies, the prayers and speeches. There was something slick about it but empty. There was nothing about the cops mowing down Keith. It got a standing O.

I stood in the back of the auditorium as the crowd filed out past Dr. Mullins, Coach, and Andy, who were accepting congratulations. Dr. Mullins and Coach were beaming like lighthouses. Andy looked miserable. He waited for everyone to leave before he came over.

"I feel like a sellout."

I'd prepared a line. "There's a second chance. *WoodhavenReal!*"

"You for real?"

"On the scoreboard at Homecoming."

He started beaming, too, then punched me. "Andiron Lives!"

The Berserkers kept their distance today, my first full practice since the concussion. Didn't break a sweat again. Didn't shower. First one out of the locker room, just in time to see Josh walking toward the parking lot. He was trying to avoid me. I pulled the truck alongside his car.

"So that's it? Show's over?" I asked.

Josh didn't have his usual energy. "We gave it our best shot."

"I don't believe in nice tries. What's spooking you?"

"Chief told me if I showed up to demonstrate he'd cancel the in-lieu-of-detention deal and have me indicted for crashing the assembly. Endangering minors. Trespassing. Inciting to riot. Other stuff."

I was winging it. "What if you didn't have to demonstrate?"

"You got a plan?"

"What if I did. You still in?"

He thought for a moment. "Maybe."

"Okay. Halftime at Homecoming. Be on the field with every-body you got. Just be there, no signs, no chants, just fill up the field like a giant mosh pit, clog it up, turn it into a human parking lot."

"Why?"

"So there's no way to get to the scoreboard."

"I can't ask my peeps to do that without telling them what's hap-pening."

"You can if they trust you."

He stared at me for a long time. "Okay."

I felt an electric surge. I spun out before the team started coming out of the locker room.

This is it for a while, Ms. L. I think I'll be too busy for regular entries. I promise to catch up eventually. Hope I have a good story to tell.

TWENTY-SEVEN

THREE NIGHTS BEFORE HOMECOMING, ANDY LOCKED the doors to his garage and transferred all our video into a new file, which he encrypted and downloaded into two external drives. I took one for safekeeping, he took one to copy and then edit. If my garage looks like a gym, his looks like a TV studio. We sat in front of a panel of monitors and we screened video, mostly shot on cell phones but even some closed-circuit TV, nanny cams, and pirated network shows. The Woodhaven kids had come through. We had amazing footage. Dr. Mullins telling a Rainbow Alliance meeting not to be so sensitive. A girl in a bathroom being groped by three guys wearing varsity football jackets. A dozen angles on The Punch. Camos rushing the stage at Keith's memorial. Berserkers hassling kids in the hallways in front of smirking coaches and teachers thumbing their phones. Ms. L talking to the football team. Me going down in 87 Gronk.

After a while, Andy leaned back in his chair, closed his eyes, and took deep breaths.

"You thinking, Lammie, or having a heart attack?"

"I'm thinking this is going to give me a heart attack."

"Scared is good," I said. "Means you're doing something worth doing. I always get an ice ball in my stomach before kickoff."

He stared at me. "Are we really sure about this? I mean there's no turning back once it goes up."

"Second thoughts?"

"It's really going to hit the fan."

"Isn't that what we want? We've been talking about it long enough."

He took a deep breath. "I didn't get to tell you. Wake Forest liked *WoodhavenStrong!* I was accepted for their workshop this summer. It could be my ticket to Stanford or NYU."

"That's great. Congrats. So what's the problem?"

"How are they going to feel when they see a second documentary that contradicts the one they liked?"

"They'll think you're a guy who can go both ways, defense and offense."

"This is no joke."

"So how do you think Division One coaches are going to feel?"

"So, are we doing too much?" I'd never seen him so serious.

Were we? "I don't think we have a choice anymore. It's the right thing to do."

Andy took more breaths. "Okay. Just how do we get it up on the scoreboard?"

"So who's the kid in charge of running video on the scoreboard?"

"Okay. But how do I keep it up there?"

"Be about five minutes before they figure out what's going on, and we should get at least another five minutes from all the kids blocking the field."

"And afterward?"

I hadn't thought that far ahead. "Doesn't matter."

"Like suspension, jail, no college, doesn't matter?"

"It's the right thing, Andy."

"How are you so sure?"

"I never felt so sure about anything."

We stared at each other. Hard. Like we were trying to look into each other's heads. Finally, he said, "You're different, man."

"Maybe."

"You always went along with the program."

"Until I didn't. Punching Kremens. The Post-it."

"Post-it?"

"When we changed rooms, Ms. L left a note for Keith. I pulled it off."

Andy let out a long breath. "I figured something like that. But not you."

"I took my eyes off the prize."

Andy thought about it, shook his head. "Maybe this is the prize."

We sat up all night spinning through the hundreds of videos, stills, and audio pieces we had collected. We took notes. If there was something we both really liked, Andy would copy it onto an external drive. We stopped only to get energy drinks and protein bars from the minifridge in the garage.

At dawn, Andy leaned back and said, "Write it."

"Write it?"

"Then I'll edit it."

It took me a few beats to realize he wasn't kidding. "I don't know how to write a documentary."

"Sure you do. We've done it. All those little pieces goofing around. Same thing. Remember, you just thread your favorite pictures together like pearls on a string."

"Where do I start?"

"With a bang," Andy said.

"How about Cogan stuffing Keith into his locker?"

"Okay. Next shot?"

"Hold on a minute. How about opening with the closing shot of *WoodHavenStrong!* Kids walking into school, smiling, the national anthem playing. Very little narration, like, *Just another sunny day at Woodhaven*. Real cheesy. Then cut to Cogan stuffing Keith into a locker."

"Sounds like a start."

Just so you don't get the wrong idea, Ms. L, the documentary was more Andy than Ron. He kept coming up with ideas for scenes that should follow each other, and he seemed to have total recall of all our footage. But I feel good about my contributions, although by the time I'm getting this down it's days later and a lot is blurry. So I'm including a copy of my rough script, which I saved on a thumb drive. It's not the final by any means but you'll get the idea. Of course, by now you've seen the doc, which is all over the place, including Facebook, Instagram, and YouTube.

COLD OPEN

```
Morning, sunny day, kids
walking into front doors of
Woodhaven High School
```

(audio: chatter [inaudible],
national anthem, pledge
of allegiance)

VOICE-OVER: Just another day
at Woodhaven High School

                              CUT TO

Football locker room. Players
are kneeling around Coach, who
is shouting, "Warriors are here
to make a difference, take a
stand, protect, and attack and
teach the world what a man can
do. And you are warriors."

INTERCUT pep talk with close-ups
of players, linger on Cogan and
Berserkers, who are red-faced and
(inaudibly) shouting back at Coach

                              CUT TO

(audio: bells ring)

Hallway as Cogan and the
Berserkers are struggling
with a kid who is trying
to get away from them.

                              SLOW REVEAL

It is Keith Korn.

                                   CUT TO

Cogan stuffs Keith into a locker.

                                   PAN TO

Teacher ignoring what's going
on, looking at his phone

                              SCREEN TO BLACK

(audio: Mahler's Fifth Symphony)

Andiron Productions

Present

WoodhavenReal!

                              DISSOLVE TO-

(audio: bells ring)

Dr. Mullins fist-bumping
kids in the halls

CUT TO

School board meeting. Mr. Kremens
is arguing against the banning of a
book about transgender teens by the
school library. He's holding up a
book called <u>Beyond Magenta</u>. "These
are true stories about real kids."

PAN TO

Somebody in the audience is
shouting down Mr. Kremens
with "This is just part of the
plot to brainwash our children
and sell perversion."

(audio: angry voices and gavel
banging dissolve into beating drum)

CUT TO

Josh marching into the auditorium,
WAAR signs, the drum

CUT TO

Confrontation with Rhino

(audio mostly inaudible, but we

do hear the chanting, "No justice
no peace, No justice no peace."

CUT TO

The Punch. Josh goes down.

CUT TO

Coach in the locker room. He is
red-faced, shaking, screaming,
"Viking warriors, you will wipe
those East Valley pussies off
the face of the earth; you
will show them who we are."

PAN TO

Cogan screaming back at him.
"Berserkers lead the way!"

CUT TO

Classroom-Rainbow Alliance
meeting with Dr. Mullins. She
is telling them not to be so
sensitive. "You're just making
yourselves into targets, provoking
them. You have to suck it up."

                                        CUT TO

A girl (face pixilated for
anonymity) in a bathroom being
groped by three guys wearing
varsity football jackets

(audio: girl sobbing,
boys laughing)

                                        CUT TO

Assembly. The vice principal is
saying, "This is not who we are."

                                SCREEN TO BLACK

(audio of rifle shots)

                            SCREEN OPENS FROM CENTER—

Conference room montage of Debate
Club kids screaming, dropping
under table, scrambling for door

(audio: Keith moaning, "I'm
sorry." Then, one shot.)

                                        CUT TO

TV footage of kids being
led out of school

                              CUT TO

An assembly. The mayor is
offering thoughts and prayers
to the injured. Dr. Mullins
appears on big screen in a
wheelchair waving her fist and
shouting, "WoodhavenStrong!"

                              CUT TO

Hospital lobby, Vikings
Against Cancer Party

                           QUICK CUTS

Party scenes, kids talking, Maddie
getting an award, various student
government kids speaking, "This
is Woodhaven, together with a
mission." Dr. Mullins live on
crutches waving her fist and
shouting, "WoodhavenStrong!"

                              CUT TO

Memorial for Keith

Josh speaking: "We're not here to
take the blame or to assign it for
the tragedy of Keith's life and
death. He was bullied in a system
that allowed it, even encouraged
it as a way to keep students under
control. He was shot to death—
unarmed—in a system that glorifies
guns as routine problem solvers.

                        INTERCUT JOSH

People in crowd with candles,
Berserkers and camos blowing
them out, fighting

                            CUT TO

Ground littered with dead candles

                    SCREEN TO BLACK

   I don't think I was ever as nervous turning in a paper to a teacher
as I was emailing the rough script to Andy. He was only a few feet
away, but he didn't even glance at me as he took his time scrolling
through it, sometimes mouthing words.
   Finally, he said, "I can make this work."

We high-fived.

"What next?"

"Get some sleep, Ron. You got to play a game." He was already flexing his fingers over his keyboard. "Scorsese time."

I got out of his way.

TWENTY-EIGHT

UP EARLY ON GAME DAY. TOOK BUTKUS ON A JOG around the neighborhood. He ran ahead but came back once he saw I was just loosening up. For an old dog he still has lots of energy. I wondered if I could take him to college. I wondered if I was going to college.

The ice ball was familiar and comforting. Not everything was different. I hoped it didn't start melting too soon.

I'm thinking, Before this day is over, most everything is going to be different. Maybe not better or worse, but different. What else is new? Life is always going to be changing, becoming different. Rhino the Philosopher speaks.

I had an egg sandwich with yogurt and applesauce. It was as much as I could get down.

The texts from the coaches started early. My cell pinged with notifications from the Vikings team chat. I checked in but didn't bother responding or even reading most of them. Same old. Maybe not the same old for me.

There were good luck texts from Josh, Ms. L, Mr. Biedermann, Joy, Tyla, even Marco. That wasn't same old.

Mom, Dad, and Livy were out of the house. We planned to meet up after the game. I wasn't so sure I'd be making it.

I talked into the journal a little, wrestled with Butkus, who seemed unusually needy today. Did he know something was up? Dogs can sense changes in the emotional atmosphere.

Feeling edgy. What if this is the end of football for me?

The ice ball begins to melt down my legs.

Yeah, what about that, Rhino?

Maybe football's not the only game I can play, Ronnie.

You really mean that or you're just covering yourself for more screwups, like The Punch and the Post-it?

You so sure they were screwups, Ronnie? It got us here.

I've been offline for a couple of days. Busy. But it's still all vivid.

By the time our team bus rolled in, the stands were packed, and the smoke was thick over the parking lot with tailgate cooking fires. Coach had kept us together as long as possible, big lunch in the cafeteria, rest, some video sessions, a light meal in a restaurant at the mall, then the ride to Lt. Neal Frischling Stadium, named for a Vikings quarterback who died in Afghanistan. Mr. Biedermann almost lost his job a couple of years ago for suggesting in class that Neal Frischling had died in vain, that the war was unnecessary, that most wars are unnecessary. More people are saying that now. What will they be saying about what we are going to do here today?

We dressed quietly, except for the Berserkers growling and pounding pads in their corner. I'm starting to hate them as much as I did in peewee.

But most people think you're one of them, Rhino; people look up to you as one of them, a football player, a real man.

Maybe not after halftime.

The coaches herd us into a kneeling circle around Coach. I hit record.

"No pep talk today, men, because you don't need one. You are warriors."

He'd said that before.

"So let me just remind you of the difference between warriors like you and the rest of the world, the everyday people, the women, the snowflakes, and the pukes. Warriors are here to make a difference, take a stand, protect and attack and teach the world what a man can do. And you are warriors."

Coach lets that sink in while I give Jamaal the wide eyes and he rolls his. He knows something is going down, he just doesn't have all the deets. Same as Josh. Andy is the only one who knows everything. I've convinced myself that I'm protecting all my friends—if things go bad, they'll have deniability. That's not true. I just don't trust anybody totally except Andy. He's the true warrior.

Coach is still talking. Can't help himself.

"Today you will find out for yourselves what you've got inside, what you're willing to sacrifice, how much you care about this game and Woodhaven and your brother warriors."

Cogan and the Berserkers were yelling back at him and then we broke and trotted out onto the field. The crowd stood and cheered down at us, waves of roars you could feel slapping against your pads.

Homecoming is always a big deal at Woodhaven, but this year was bigger, an army reserve color guard, lots more police cars, county and state. There was a standing O for Dr. Mullins, who walked out on the field waving a WOODHAVENSTRONG! banner. A couple of the kids who had been wounded were standing with her. There were a few speeches. I didn't pay attention. I waved to Dad, Mom, and Livy. Cogan kept glaring at me.

Cogan and the rest of the seniors pranced as the PA announcer called their names. Pranced like show horses. Our mascot Thor slapped them on the butt with his foam hammer as they lined up. Perlick kicked Thor in the nuts. Big Berserker laugh and Cogan high-fived Perlick. The last of the ice ball drained and warmed up. Now I had a stomachache as I lined up with the rest of the team along our sideline.

One of the kids who had been shot sang the national anthem.

I guess I wasn't paying total attention because I didn't look down the line until the crowd started booing.

Jamaal had taken a knee. Justin and a couple other Black guys kneeled with him. Domi stood behind Jamaal and put a hand on his shoulder, the only white guy in the group.

Jamaal looked at me, a challenging stare with his eyebrows raised. *You with me, brother?*

I punked out, looked away. I'm with you, brother, but not right now. Eyes on the prize. A different prize today. Can't do anything until I help Andy get *WoodhavenReal!* on the scoreboard. Can't risk getting yanked now.

I tried to stay away from Jamaal on the sideline, but we ended up a few yards away at the kickoff. I could read his lips.

"Better be good." He knew something was up.

I nodded. It was good. Just how good I didn't find out till after it was all over. I never got a chance to see the finished doc before it went up.

Coach started the seniors, an old Homecoming tradition. He didn't play Jamaal at all that first half, punishment for taking the knee. Maybe he hoped he wouldn't need Jamaal. Justin and Domi didn't get much playing time either. I was in and out of the game, mostly as an outside linebacker.

A scoreless game. For all the Berserker noise, they struggled to shut down the Port Hampton offense. Near the end of the half, the Porters were on our fifteen-yard line, first down. They clearly had the momentum to score when Coach Colligan called the suicide blitz, which was pretty ballsy and maybe a little reckless when the game wasn't on the line yet. Turned out to be a brilliant move. Or just lucky.

Their quarterback read the play. Something about his body language told me that. In a suicide blitz every defender charges the quarterback, and if he doesn't read it right away, he'll get swamped, maybe go down for a big loss, even lose the ball. If he does read it and drops back fast enough, he can pick his target—his receivers will all be uncovered.

He read it. He was set to burn us.

I remembered from films the way this quarterback usually rolled left, faked, then spun to his right to pass when the play was going to his favorite wideout. From the way he was swiveling his feet, I had the feeling he was going to do that again, a quick release before the blitz got to him. We were out of the huddle, the crowd was screaming "DEE-FENSE," there was no way for me to shout a warning that could be heard.

So I hung back two steps on the blitz and sidestepped to my left. I was directly in front of the wideout when we both reached for the pass.

I thought, Rhino's Run.

It was just too high for me to catch. As I touched it with my fingertips, I spotted Cogan a few steps to my right and tipped it toward him. He pulled it into his chest and took off.

I was alongside him. "Go, go, go," I yelled.

He lowered his head and plunged downfield.

I'm not fast but Cogan was slower so I could keep up with him easily, running shotgun, watching out for the speedy Porter backs who could catch up with us. A little running back came up behind Cogan. I dropped back a step, turned, and shouldered him into the sidelines. When I caught up with Cogan we were on our forty-yard line. He grinned and nodded. Sixty yards to go.

He was already slowing down. I heard his breathing, even louder and raspier than mine. It sounded like synchronized gasping, two big heavy guys running for their lives on lungs and legs that weren't built for the sprint. We were on the Port Hampton forty.

Another speedy back coming out of nowhere. He was reaching for Cogan, who was sucking for air. If he even tapped Cogan, he would probably topple over. I juked left and rammed my shoulder into his chest. I almost went down with him.

I was staggering, lungs bursting, lifting my lead legs with my core. A stitch ran up my left side. When I caught up with Cogan again our eyes met. We were on the twenty.

The wide receiver I'd beaten for the pick was on the other side of Cogan now with a perfect angle for a tackle. He was gathering speed while we were slowing down. We had nothing left. No way Cogan could avoid him.

I found the last ounce and let myself collide with the wide receiver. Actually, I just staggered into him. We both went down.

Cogan stumbled on. I was on my hands and knees when he crossed the goal line, spiked the ball, and threw up his arms.

Then he wobbled back to me, helped me up. We threw our arms around each other. "Awesome," he said. At that moment, I loved Cogan, he was my brother, we were what the game was all about.

TWENTY-NINE

THE TEAM WAS ON TOP OF US, POUNDING HELMETS and pads. The coaches pushed us onto the sideline before we got a delay penalty. Belfer made the extra point. The score was 7–0 when the half ended. It felt like we had won the game.

I got swept into the locker room, everybody yelling and bouncing, Jamaal and Domi close. I sagged against them until I was breathing regularly.

Cogan and I couldn't stop grinning at each other.

The coaches and trainers started moving around us, words I didn't hear, water bottles, checking injuries and tapings.

It took me a few minutes to float back to Earth, to remember that I still needed to make my move. Rhino's Run wasn't over.

If I still wanted to do it.

I looked around the room. The team was way up, sky high, ready to dominate the second half and win. What about me? I was vibrating with electrical energy, the reason I was here in the first place, why football was number one in my life, surrounded by my brothers, including Cogan. I was happy and safe here.

Did I really want to give this all up?

Andy caught my eye, made a little motion with his head toward the TV on the wall. The local station that broadcast the game had the halftime show on. Suddenly, Josh and a mob of kids filled the screen, marching onto the field, right into the band and the cheerleaders. There were more than a hundred of them, the WAAR kids leading, but lots of other kids, too, other schools. I spotted Tyla and Joy near the front. It was just what I had asked Josh to do without telling him what I was going to do. He had delivered big-time. He trusted me. Now what?

"Look at this," Cogan yelled.

The Berserkers clustered under the TV, yelling at it.

I saw Andy slip out of the locker room, his laptop under his arm.

I whispered to Jamaal, "Gotta get back out."

"Wassup?"

"You did good. My turn now."

"What are you going to do?" he asked.

"Bring your guys out to the scoreboard."

I waited until most of the team and coaches were crowded under the TV before I wrapped a Vikings windbreaker over my uniform and pulled the hood tight around my head.

I walked out of the locker room, then jogged toward the scoreboard. People were coming down from the stands. Some joined Josh's crowd, others started yelling at them, shoving them. I ran through the mob, head down.

Andy was squatting in the small equipment shed behind the scoreboard, his laptop balanced on his knees. I crouched next to him.

"How we doing?"

"Almost ready," he said, and stabbed the keyboard. There was a loud pop and the sounds of shattering glass. "An overload. Afraid of that."

I leaned out of the shed and looked up at the scoreboard. "Just a couple bulbs blew."

"Yeah, but they'll come to fix it," Andy said.

Two groundskeepers were already hurrying toward us, pointing at the exploded lights.

"Here they come."

"Keep 'em away."

I waited until they crossed the goal line before I stepped out to meet them.

"Rhino! Great blocks. What are you doing here?"

"A surprise presentation," I said.

"No one told us."

"It's a surprise."

"Gotta change those bulbs. Spares in the shed. Hey, what's he doing in there?"

Andy looked up, shot me two fingers. He needed two more minutes.

They were average-sized guys, older than Dad, out of shape. I could keep them occupied for a few minutes, but fighting them, even just pushing them around, wasn't something I wanted to do.

"We just need a couple minutes, guys," I said. "Can you give me that?"

They looked at each other and nodded. One of them pulled a pen and a to-do pad out of his overalls pocket. "You sign this for me, Rhino? Be valuable when you win the Super Bowl."

I stepped in front of Andy to obscure their view of him. "Glad to. Especially the Super Bowl part."

I kept grinning and took my time. "Who knew Cogan could run like that? What a guy."

"Long run for a big fella," said one of the groundskeepers.

"Tell me about it. Still catching my breath."

They laughed and the other one held out a pen and paper. I gave him a slow scrawl.

"Glad you guys keep the turf so hard. Never would have made it on mud."

One of them glanced over his shoulder at the crowd filling the field. "Where are the cops? If they don't clear the field soon it'll be all chewed up."

I was handing him his paper back when a sudden blast of noise rocked us.

It was the national anthem coming from the scoreboard as kids walked into school on a sunny day.

My voice: *Just another day at Woodhaven High School.*

We were up!

One of the groundskeepers said, "What the hell's that?"

Coach was screaming... *you are warriors.*

I glanced back and forth between the screen and the crowd on the field. They were turning toward the scoreboard, pointing, freezing in place. Players started coming out of the locker room.

ANDIRON PRODUCTIONS PRESENT
WOODHAVENREAL!

Mr. Kremens filled the screen. "These are true stories about real kids."

There's squawking from a groundskeeper's pocket. He pulls out a radio, says, "Yeah, we're right here. Rhino, too." He looks at Andy. "You better shut that off."

I step between Andy and the groundskeepers again. "Just another minute or so."

"School know about this?"

On screen, Keith is moaning, "I'm sorry."

"Almost over," I say.

The groundskeepers are lunging at Andy. I manage to block one of them, but the other one gets past me. Andy snaps the laptop shut and protects it with his body as he gets slammed down.

People are overrunning us. I pull the groundskeeper off Andy, Jamaal pulls someone off me. Where'd he come from? I'm under a pileup, grateful for my pads, wish I had my helmet, then I'm in the middle of a tug-of-war. Marco pulls me loose.

I crawl away to get one last look as the screen freezes on the dead candles after Keith's memorial, then someone sends me sprawling. It's Perlick, Cogan right behind him. I guess our brotherhood is over. He's drawing his fist back as Belfer grabs my arms from behind. I brace for Cogan's punch, no way to dodge it, but it never lands.

Josh is hanging on Cogan's arm, dragging it down. Josh's peeps are wrapping themselves around football players twice their size. I feel like cheering. Whistles are blowing. Now I see the cops.

Tyla and Joy are peeling people off Andy. With Jamaal and Justin, they make a pocket around Andy, start hustling him away. Cogan breaks loose from Josh and elbows him in the gut. Josh flies backward, lands hard on the ground. Cogan kicks him in the ribs twice. He stops to admire his work, then pulls back his leg to aim a kick at Josh's head. Mr. Biedermann shoulders Cogan, who's off balance and goes down. Then Mr. Biedermann pulls me away and we follow Andy out of the stadium.

The PA announcer is shouting something I can't make out.

Andy catches my eye. His nose and mouth are bleeding, but he looks happy. He's shouting at me. It takes me awhile to figure out what he's saying. "We did it."

We did it.

What did we do?

THIRTY

MR. BIEDERMANN IS HERDING US TOWARD THE PARKING lot, yelling, "Go, go, go." Behind us, hundreds of people are milling on the field, a monster mosh pit. People are shouting at the screen, which has started showing the film over again from the beginning. People are yelling and cursing and laughing and high-fiving and shaking their heads at the scoreboard. I wanted to go back and listen to what they were saying, but it was time to get out because cops were flooding the zone, not just local cops, but reinforcements from other towns, also county and state police. How had so many shown up so fast? Were they waiting somewhere close, was the chief expecting trouble? He was the one making trouble, leading the charge, shoving and kicking, swinging a baton, turning this into a riot. I started to go back, but Mr. Biedermann had a tight grip on my shoulder pads through the windbreaker. "Just keep moving, Ron."

Andy caught my eye. "Hope somebody's shooting this." He wanted to go back, too.

Bullhorns were blaring now. "Clear the field, clear the field immediately."

Mr. Biedermann stuffs us into his old Chevy van. He gets behind the wheel. Josh stays outside the van. He slams the doors shut and slaps a fender, yelling, "Move it." Then he turns to face the mob rushing toward us. It's a movie scene. Heroic Josh. I try to get out of the car, can't leave Josh behind, but Andy and Tyla pull me back. Then Mr. Biedermann is blasting out of the parking lot.

"What about the game?" Justin yelled.

Jamaal laughed. "The game is o-vah."

"They'll call it," Andy said.

"They'll call it a riot," Tyla said. "They had all those cops ready. They knew something was going to happen."

Mr. Biedermann drove us to his house, a dumpy old ranch on the edge of town. He rented it after his marriage broke up. The inside was kind of messy, books and free weights scattered, but comfortable. A monster couch in front of a huge TV. Andy, Jamaal, and I hit the couch, Justin climbed on the stationary bike.

"First thing, guys," Mr. Biedermann said. "Call or text your parents, let them know you're all right. They can pick you up, or I can get you home or back to the parking lot."

Andy found the local TV news channel. They were broadcasting live. People were still on the field. The chief looked pleased with himself. "We've detained seventeen people, disorderly conduct, resisting arrest—this is not Woodhaven, these are radicals from out of town."

The reporter holding the mic just nodded at him, then turned to Cogan, his face bloody but grinning. "That was an amazing run, John."

"Berserkers rule!" he shouted.

Mr. Biedermann broke out soda and chips. We were all hungry. He ordered pizza. He was very calm. "Okay, guys, I figure the cops are going to be here soon. We need to talk."

"Get our stories straight?" Jamaal asked.

"No, just think about what you want to say. Tell the truth. But don't say too much. There'll be lawyers. There'll be lots of media. You all sent your texts?" When we all nodded, he said, "You all made me very proud today. I think you woke up a lot of people."

"People only going to believe what they already believe," said Jamaal. "Like preaching to the choir."

"Maybe," said Mr. Biedermann. "But you have to keep the choir brave, too. By the way, Jamaal, that was very gutsy."

He shrugged. "If Kaepernick can do it . . ."

Flashing lights outside the house. Everybody's cell went off at once, the school emergency siren. A cop voice blared, "The house is surrounded. Come out one at a time, hands over your head." I thought it was a prank at first, but I couldn't figure out who was pulling it.

It was real. Surreal.

Andy was on his knees, shooting on his cell through a front window. Over his head I could see the cop car lights.

"Everybody stay down," Mr. Biedermann said, going to the door. When he opened it, a bullhorn bellowed, "Throw out your weapons."

Mr. Biedermann yelled, "For God's sake, just kids in here, no guns . . ."

"Hands over your head. Come out slowly."

"It's on TV," Andy yelled. "It's all on TV." He was shifting his cell phone back and forth between the window and the big TV.

Out the windows, I could see cop cars and TV cameras.

On the big screen in the house, I could see the house, Mr. Biedermann, hands up, framed in the doorway, and Andy at the window, shooting.

The bullhorn bellowed again, "Tear gas."

I pulled Andy away from the window just before the first canister crashed through.

Mr. Biedermann turned back to us, but we were shoving him out the door, coughing and crying. The tear gas stung; it felt like little hot flakes scratching my eyeballs. Tyla was holding my arm, her face buried in my side, and I was dragging her and Andy out into the fresh air.

THIRTY-ONE

THEY CANCELED THE SECOND HALF OF THE HOMECOM-
ing game and the next week's game for "safety concerns," and
there've been all kinds of public meetings at Town Hall, the school,
the church, for and against firing Coach and Dr. Mullins and bringing charges against Andy and me. Donald Trump was quoted saying
Andy and I should go to jail, and Colin Kaepernick said we should
get a medal. And then four kids died in a school shooting in Califor-
nia and our story disappeared.

I guess you followed all this, Ms. L, even though you never
answered my emails and texts, which just means I'll have to head
up to Buffalo after a visit with Alison, whose old dog shelter is on
the same route north. I need to thank her in person for those magic
words, "There you go."

So, yeah, I'm glad we did it, although Andy and I are still trying
to figure out just what we actually did and if anything happened
that mattered, that changed things. He thinks it's too early to tell.

Some people woke up, some people stuck their heads deeper in the ground. Josh agrees with that but says we have to look ahead, not behind. Keep marching.

One thing I learned from Mr. Biedermann is how important history is, how context shapes what happens. The past helps explain the present. What would have been different if I had stepped up when Cogan bullied Keith? Would Keith be alive?

Tyla says I shouldn't beat myself up about that. The past is past. She thinks Andy and I did a good thing and should keep looking for more good things to do. We've been hanging out. She works nights at a nursing home. She wants to be a therapist. She'll be a good one.

It's eight days to the election and that's all anyone is talking about now. Mr. Kremens says Hillary is a shoo-in to win while Dad thinks Trump has a good chance. In fact, he says he was planning to vote for him against "that crooked woman" until he trashed Andy and me. Whatever you think, Sarge is still my dad.

Woodhaven seems divided on the election, also on what should happen next in town. The rumor is that a deal is going down where Dr. Mullins and Coach retire for "health reasons" and that I'm off the team for the rest of this season but will be allowed to come back in the fall. Same for Jamaal and Justin and the other kids who knelt. Andy loses his job as sports video director. No charges filed against us or any other student, including Josh and Cogan. Mr. Kremens and Dad have been negotiating with the mayor.

Alison said those sound like "real world" decisions, ambiguous compromises that don't satisfy anybody but which people can live with. That word again, *ambiguity*.

Mr. Biedermann was fired, but lawyers from the city are fighting it. He seems positive about the whole thing. He told Andy and me he liked *WoodhavenReal!* He would have given it an A minus. It might have been even more powerful, he said, if it was more focused on one issue, like gun control or censorship or bullying. Andy said we'll keep that in mind for the streaming series.

Dad talks about my "sacrifice"—giving up football for the rest of the season as being like Ali not being allowed to box for three years—as if I had made a conscious choice. He says it will make me stronger. I'm not sure about that.

Mom is worried that all the publicity will lower real estate values and cut into her commissions. Livy wonders what Woodhaven High will be like when she gets there in the fall. She was counting on having a big shot senior jock brother; now she's afraid I might quit football and hang out with dorks and nerds.

I still love football, but I have been eating lunch lately with Tyla, Joy, and Marco. It's fun, they're smart, and who else can I talk to about Group and our journals?

Turns out, Marco has a lot to say and he's the only person who asked me about how I felt blocking for Cogan's touchdown. I told him about my dream of Rhino's Run, and how if you love football that dream still sort of came true. We scored! Then I talked him into working out with me for next season. He's only a sophomore and the offensive line could use him.

Joy wants to stay with gymnastics, but it's not clear if she'll be allowed to join the girls' team. Andy thinks that could be an entire episode in the new doc. He's already working on a rough outline.

If you assume Josh and I came out of this big bros like our dads, you haven't been reading carefully. He's a good enough guy, I suppose, on the right side of most things, but he's still a stuck-up jerk who imagines himself a superior human being. He's Josh Kremens and you're not. That voice! I should have punched him in the throat. On the other hand, he did come through in the clutch. Don't think he doesn't remind me.

He plans a gap year to travel abroad before going to Harvard or Yale. Just the way he says "ah-broad" scrapes my teeth. He thinks I should take a year off, too, before I go to some football factory.

It's not a bad idea. Maybe I'll write a book that year. I've got most of what happened already written. And gain twenty pounds of muscle before college. And figure out what just happened and how I *feel* about it. Isn't that what it's all about, Ms. L?

ACKNOWLEDGMENTS

Sixty years ago, when I was a sports reporter for the *New York Times*, an editor from Harper & Row, Ferdinand Monjo, sent me a letter asking if I would write a book with "boxing as its milieu." That book, *The Contender*, which is still in print, was the first of thirteen Young Adult novels of mine published by what is now HarperCollins.

I'm deeply grateful for all the helping Harper hands along the way, including people in marketing, sales, library services, production, publicity, and administration, many of whom I never met but nevertheless cherish for their expertise and hard work in the cause of reading. I have unbounded appreciation and adoration for the ones I worked with most closely—my editors—from Ferdie, my first editor; his boss, Ursula Nordstrom, who invented the YA genre; Charlotte Zolotow, the most exquisite of editors; Robert Warren, Ruth Katcher, and the brilliant starting quarterback on this book, Ben Rosenthal, and his sturdy replacement, David Linker. Thank you all for the best sixty years of this writing life.